Bournemouth 90

Billy Morris

ISBN: 9798465002691

Print Edition

Copyright 2021 Billy Morris

All Rights reserved. No part of this book may be reproduced in any form without the prior permission of the author.

The characters and events in this book are fictitious. Any similarity to real persons, living or dead, is coincidental and not intended by the author.

The author can be contacted at BM.Author@outlook.com

Billy Morris was born in Leeds, Yorkshire in 1966. He left Leeds in the late 1990's and has lived and worked in Europe and USA. He now lives in the Philippines. Bournemouth 90 is his first book.

Accents, Dialects and Pronunciation

Bournemouth 90 is set in Leeds, a city in West Yorkshire in the North of England. The Leeds accent could generally be described as 'Yorkshire' but is quite distinct, and is easily identifiable when compared to speech in other parts of the county. Even different areas of the city have their own distinct dialects.

People in Leeds have a tendency to miss out letters, join words together and speak quite quickly. It's not an exaggeration to say that a conversation between Leeds folk could sound like a foreign language when compared to 'BBC English.'

Including dialogue exactly as it would most likely be spoken would therefore make this book unreadable for many people. However, there are certain fundamental elements of the Leeds accent which I felt needed to be reflected, in order to maintain a level of authenticity in the characters' speech. The following substitutions have therefore been made throughout the book-

The most obvious is the dropping of the word 'the' before a noun. In Leeds 'the' will be replaced by what linguists call a glottal stop. Execution of this element of the Leeds accent is generally difficult for a non-Yorkshire native. Actors on TV and in films usually get it wrong by either missing out 'the' entirely, or pronouncing a 't' in its place. As a Leeds speaker, I can't even explain how to execute a glottal stop. Google tells me it's achieved by rapidly closing the vocal chords. I've no idea how you do that. If you want to hear an example, I suggest you listen to an interview with David Batty or Kalvin Phillips. They're both experts. In the book, a glottal stop to replace 'the' is denoted by an apostrophe (').

"We're going to the pub' would therefore become "We're off to' pub".

Owt, Nowt and Summat – The words anything, nothing and something will usually be replaced by owt, nowt and summat by a native Leeds speaker. Owt is pronounced 'oat', nowt is pronounced 'note', summat is 'summert'.

I recognise it may be confusing to include speech patterns which are unrecognisable beyond the boundaries of West Yorkshire, but I felt that dialect would become unrealistic in the context of the story without at least including these substitutions. I hope this doesn't impact on your enjoyment of the book.

Chapter 1

Monday 9th April 1990

The knot in Neil Yardsley's stomach tightened as the train lurched to halt. New Pudsey. Nearly home. Back in an LS postcode for the first time in three years. No grand homecoming today though. He'd avoided the Trans-Pennine mainline which sped past the futuristic Systime building on the Ring Road and the tallest floodlights in Europe, before pulling into the station and its sign which read 'Welcome to Leeds. A Fine City. Home to Joshua Tetley's Brewery since 1822.'

Today he'd slipped in through the back door. Taking the first train from Lime Street to Manchester, changing at Victoria, then on past the rain soaked hills and derelict mills of East Lancashire and West Yorkshire. Todmorden, Hebden Bridge, Mytholmroyd, Sowerby Bridge, Brighouse. Tall chimneys, cobbled streets, Last of the Summer Wine and Asian sweatshops. Then rattling past the back gardens and industrial estates of West Leeds. Pudsey, Bramley, Armley, Wortley. LS28, 13 and 12, then the familiar sight of the city skyline and the 18 platforms of City Station. Head down, through the barriers, self conscious in his court suit, too tight after three years of Walton nick's shit food and twenty three hour bang-up, which had recently become a full lockdown in response to the prison riots sweeping the country.

Heart thumping as he handed his ticket over at the barrier and headed across the concourse, past WH Smiths and Boots, towards the City Arms, and the old Yorkshire Post vendor sat like a gnome on a stool next to the station door. Five pence more than the last one he'd bought, but Neil handed over the 22p and was passed a folded broadsheet which immediately covered his fingers in smudged newsprint. His first YEP in three years. A daily ritual since his first day at work nine years earlier, and one which meant he was finally home. Back in the string of beads. As always, straight to the back page for Don Water's United report.

'Forget it, Wilkinson tells angry Strachan -- Howard Wilkinson will wait to see referee John Martin's report before deciding whether to take any action against Gordon Strachan following his skipper's angry outburst at the end of Saturday's draw with Bradford City.'

Neil glanced at the front page before folding the paper and tucking it under his arm.

Soldiers Killed by Land Mine -- Four soldiers were killed today in a massive terrorist landmine explosion in Northern Ireland which blew their Land Rover off the road outside Downpatrick, Co Down.

Everything the same, but feeling different. Down the steps and a sharp right opposite the Scarborough Taps. Doors locked and Monday morning shoppers dodging Saturday night pavement stains. Under the tunnel dripping dark oily water from the tracks above, and a chill wind whipping in behind the cars queuing from the M621. Out past the Dragonara, now re-invented as the Hilton, Revie's carpet bowls and bingo nights long forgotten. Pace quickening past Fletcher's garage and memories of forecourt stock trashed in the cross-fire, as the Headhunters' double-deckers had got caught in post-match traffic a few years earlier.

Gypsy caravans on Holbeck Moor in the shadow of his mother's high rise. Neil Yardsley looked up to the 8th floor, took a deep breath and opened the door. The smell of Dettol just about overcoming piss, but no lights in the lift meaning an eight flight climb. Panting, out of shape, he paused before knocking. 'Mum I'm home'. But it wasn't his home. Never had been, never would be. And for her, this was as much a prison cell as the one he'd just left eighty miles away in Liverpool.

Three knocks, feeling awkward. He'd not seen her for 18 months. Not since the emphysema had squeezed the last gasps of air from her lungs and confined her to a box in the sky, gulping oxygen from a metal bottle like a fish on a riverbank.

"Mam?" The hallway seemed narrower than he'd remembered. The radiator blasting out heat, and a smell that reminded him of his Nan's back-to-back in Woodhouse.

"Hi. You must be Neil?" The girl was his age, mid twenties, dark bobbed hair framing the pretty face of a teenager. A blue medical tunic over black leggings concealed her figure, and a pair of round glasses gave her a studious air. She looked like a primary school teacher, but after three years without speaking to a girl, he suddenly felt like a twelve year old at a school disco, plucking up courage to ask for a dance.

"Erm...yes. Neil. I've...hello."

"I'm Julie. I'm Christine's helper. I come in every day to sort her out." The girl turned and headed towards a door on the left. "She's in here."

He'd been preparing himself for this moment for the last month, since he was told his parole had been granted, but now it had arrived he just wanted to be somewhere else. Anywhere but here, in this tiny room on the 8th floor of a Holbeck tower block, with its gas fire burning three bars, its smell of decay and hospitals and a view through the window of burning tyres and a motorway.

"Hello mam, you alright?" The stupidity of the question was apparent to them both as she forced a smile and tears began to trickle down the rubber mask wrapped round her cheeks.

"I'm alright love. Just got this bloody thing on all day now." She looked small and defeated. An old lady in her mid forties.

"I'm sorry Neil..."

"Don't be daft, why are you sorry?"

"I couldn't come anymore. I couldn't get transport and the lifts here are never working. I'm sorry love..." Her sobs dissolved into rasping croaks as she gasped for air and shook her head.

"You've nowt to be sorry about mam. I'm the one should be sorry." He thought he detected a nod from Julie as she fiddled with the oxygen bottle.

"Try not to get upset Christine, it makes it harder for you to breathe. Neil's home now."

"You are home aren't you? I mean, you plan to stop at your mum's?" It sounded more like a direction than a question.

"Well, I intended to, at least for a bit. You said in your letter Stu has moved out?" He turned back to his mother.

"Couple of months back. He's sharing a house with Danno in Headingley somewhere. I've not been there but he pops round a few times a week. Have you heard from him?"

"Not for a few weeks." More like a few months, but he didn't want his mother to know that his brother's last visit had ended in him leaving after fifteen minutes with a parting comment of 'Fuck you, you loser.'

"Have you got a phone number or address for him?"

"There should be a number on' pad by' phone. Pass us it here Julie."

Julie handed over the notebook and flicked her head towards the kitchen. Neil followed her from the room and noticed his palms were sweating as she faced him across the small dining table.

"Your mum is very ill. She gets out of breath really quickly and there's no way she can get down the stairs. I keep reporting the lift and the council fix it, but it usually breaks down again within a few days. Your brother comes round and brings her shopping and stuff, but it will be good for you to be here."

"Of course. I need to get a job though, so I won't be around all the time."

"I get that, but you've been away a long time. Just spend some time with her." Julie's obvious impatience tightened the knot in Neil's stomach and he was surprised at how much her disapproval upset him.

"Here's my number. If your mum needs anything or you're worried about her, just give me a call."

Chapter 2

'Julie Statham, Home Care Nurse, 0532 451687'. Neil lay on the small single bed and turned the card in his fingers. He'd been back less than twelve hours and already knew this wasn't going to work. No job, no money, no home. In bed at 9pm, listening to Barrymore camping it up on Strike it Lucky from next doors TV wasn't how he'd hoped to spend his first night of freedom. Stu hadn't turned up and there was no answer on the number his mother had given him. The bedroom walls reflected the fact that this had been his younger brother's room until recently.

A framed picture of the 1972 cup winning team took pride of place above the bed, even though Stu had only been a toddler when Sniffer Clarke had put the ball in the Arsenal net with his famous diving header. A mirror featuring the LUFC smiley badge logo and a list of club honours was on the opposite wall above a poster advertising Kaos at Ricky's on Merrion Street. On the wall behind the door was a 1970's silk scarf bearing the overly optimistic words 'Adamson's Aces', which Neil recognised as a souvenir from his brother's first Leeds game in 1978. Below that, an image of the 1974 Championship team giving their customary pre-match centre-circle wave in their Admiral tracksuit tops. The fact that all the memorabilia on display was more than ten years old highlighted the fact that Leeds United had been in seemingly terminal decline for most of Stuart's time as a fan.

Neil spotted a familiar A4 folder on a chest of drawers beside the door, and hauled himself from the low bed to retrieve it. He opened the file to reveal a bundle of tattered newspaper clippings. At the top of the pile were

Yorkshire Evening post clippings covering some rare, recent near-misses in the 1987 play off final and the loss to Coventry in the FA Cup semi of the same year. Below those were newspaper headlines which were more typical for Leeds in the 1980's.

'Keegan KO'd by missile.'

'Leeds Face Record Ban.'

'United Fans in Terror Rampage.'

'Night of Shame.'

Neil flicked through the clippings covering days and nights that he remembered too well- West Brom, Chelsea, Barnsley, Derby, Bradford, before pausing at a page clipped from the News of the World.

'Meet the Nastiest Crowd in the Land-- They go to football matches to fight. If there's nobody to battle with, they'll watch the game, but they think watching is for wallies. The swaggering young thugs call themselves the Service Crew after the early morning service trains they take to away games.'

Neil smiled at the memory of the bullshit fed to journalists in the early 80's. The fact was that anyone who said they were in the Service Crew, definitely wasn't, as the name was only used jokingly by those who were really in-the-know.

Next to the headline, a crowd of young men in Adidas trainers and golf jumpers grinned and did their best to look hard on a station platform. One of the faces was circled in biro and beside the circle, scrawled in childish handwriting were the words 'Our kid!'

Neil looked at the photo and recalled the day it was taken seven years earlier at Leeds station, as he and his mates had made their way to a cup game at Arsenal. He also remembered the bollocking he'd received from his mother when she'd found out that his 13 year old brother had taken the paper to school to proudly show his friends and teacher.

Turning to the following paper in the file, he knew what was coming next.

'Riot Fans Caged' from the Sun. *'The first of 125 fans arrested during rioting at the 2nd division game between Birmingham City and Leeds United appeared at Birmingham City magistrates today'*. Neil scanned the list of names, with addresses in Solihull and Sparkbrook until he located a familiar passage. *'Neil Yardsley, 20, house painter, of Beeston, Leeds was described as a ringleader who orchestrated violence on the day of the game. He was jailed for 18 months.'*

There had been plenty of press coverage of Birmingham, and Stuart had saved every report covering the riot and trial. Neil had no need to read them again, he knew the story only too well, and skimmed through the cuttings until he reached a folded tabloid at the bottom of the file. Its pages were less tattered than the others. In fact, it looked like it had never been read. Neil unfolded the cover and once again stared into his own eyes, below a headline on the front page of the Liverpool Echo – *'Armed Raid Gang Jailed.'*

Chapter 3

Tuesday 10th April 1990

450 Prison Rioters Surrender – One of the four sieges taking place at prisons around the country ended today when 450 rioting inmates gave themselves up at Bristol. Warders had been forced to evacuate three of the five wings at the city's Horfield jail after inmates ran amok on Sunday night. It is believed a hard core of 32 prisoners, moved earlier from trouble-hit Dartmoor were behind the initial outbreak at Bristol.

With names like Pleasant Place and Recreation Street, it was clear that the Victorian builders of the red brick terraced streets bordering the Britannia pub in Holbeck had a sense of humour. Neil put down the YEP and nervously scanned the door as he tried to make his pint last. His mother had lent him a tenner on the basis that Hursty had said he could get him a job, and Hursty's office was the Brit. They'd arranged to meet at five, and Neil had found himself pacing the bedroom half an hour before that, having spent the previous hour deciding what to wear. He couldn't forget the piss-taking he'd suffered last time he came out of the nick. On that occasion he'd turned up in Jacomelli's in the same gear he'd been wearing at St Andrews – Adidas Jeans trainers, 18' Lois flared cords, an M&S crew neck and a tweed jacket that one of the lads had lifted from Schofields. After the initial backslaps and handshakes, he'd noticed everyone looking him up and down, before Jacko had said 'fucking hell Yards, have you just ram-raided Oxfam?' They'd all pissed themselves laughing and he'd realised that a year was a long time in terrace fashion. Everyone was wearing bigger trainers, Nikes and New Balance seemed popular, and the flares had been replaced by looser fitting jeans by Chevignon and Ball. The dress-down look was clearly long gone, with M&S jumpers replaced by Armani, and Harris Tweed by brightly coloured Italian jackets with a strange compass badge on the arm.

A few years earlier, Neil had taken great delight in laughing at the undercover plod who always turned up to shadow the Leeds lads on Bank Holidays in Blackpool. In August they'd taken careful note of the fashions, and arrived the following Easter kitted out in bleached jeans, pringles and Fila tracksuit tops. Unfortunately for them, the look had shifted to Peter Storm Kagools, flares and hush puppies. On that day in Jacomelli's, Neil had known exactly how they'd felt.

Hursty always had the latest gear, so meeting him before the rest of the lads would give him an idea of what everyone was wearing. It was nearly three years since he'd been to a match so it wouldn't have been a surprise to see his old mate stride in wearing a cowboy hat and a kilt. Instead, the familiar grinning face with two days growth of beard, bounded through the door in double denim with a pair of thick soled Timberland moccasins, chanting 'Yards is back, Yards is back, hello! hello!' causing an old man at the bar to look up from rolling a wire thin cigarette and shake his head.

"Looking well, mate! How did' scousers treat you then?'

"I survived pal, but not summat I ever plan to do again."

"Two pints of Lowenbrau please love." Hursty was still smiling, clearly in the mood to celebrate. "Looks like you've put a bit of timber on there mate. Too much porridge eh?"

"Yeah cheers, just what I need to hear. Its not easy keeping in shape when you only get half an hour's exercise a day. I've missed this though." Neil raised his glass and smiled as he swigged off the remainder of his pint.

"Looks like Leeds are doing well - that Wilkinson seems to have sorted them out?"

"Tell you what Yards, he's really shaken things up. Got them fitter, playing like a team. Tough game tonight at Plymouth though, then Oldham on Good Friday. Could do without playing them at' minute, we never get owt there. When was' last time you went?"

"Sheff United away, February 87 was my last game."

"Lively day. When it kicked off by' ice rink wasn't it?"

"That was it. Madness. Finished with all that now mate."

"Yeah? Sticking to armed robbery are you?"

"Fuck off! I can't afford for any of that to happen again, I've got a bloody probation officer checking up on me. Need to help my mam, get a place of my own and a job sorted. That's where you come in, I hope..."

"Do I look like' job centre?" Hursty smiled and took a gulp of his pint. "We haven't got a lot going pal, but if you want it, I can sort you a driving job. Delivering car parts. Piece of piss."

"How much?"

"Six quid an hour."

"Jesus. Won't go far that..." Neil grimaced, knowing that beggars couldn't be choosers and on this occasion he was the one with his hand out.

"Cash in hand though. Off ' books. Also, it's mad busy. You could probably do fifteen hours a day, seven days a week if you wanted."

"Sounds alright till I get summat else. Thanks a lot Hursty mate, I owe you one." Neil forced a smile, not wanting to appear ungrateful.

"Plus you get to use' van whenever you want. Start tomorrow if you want?"

"Good for me. Hope I get Bank Holiday Monday off...Blades at home isn't it?"

"Sorted you on that score too." Hursty smiled as he opened his wallet and tossed a ticket across the table.

"Twelve quid? Lowfields seats? Is that where everyone goes now?"

"Not usually, but we've heard the BBC have bought a load of tickets for there. Could be interesting..."

"Nah, they never turn up at Elland Road." Neil shook his head, secretly hoping Sheffield's hooligan firm wouldn't prove him wrong on this occasion.

"We'll see eh? Seen your kid yet?"

"No, I've been trying to get hold of him. Why?"

"Nowt." Hursty slurped down his pint. "Same again?"

"Yeah. What made you ask about our kid?"

"Probably nowt. Just summat I heard." Hursty shouted over his shoulder as he headed to the bar.

"What did you hear then?" Neil got the feeling that Hursty wished he hadn't raised the subject as he sat back down.

"One of ' lads said he's working for Connolly, not sure if it's right. I wouldn't worry about it mate."

"Connolly?"

"Yeah, mental old bastard, has' Waterloo in Harehills. Takes orders off his brother who's been dead for ten years. Runs all' drugs in town now, guns in Chapeltown, you name it..."

"I know who he is. Who said that about our Stuart?"

"One of ' lads. Can't remember who. It's probably bollocks. We're meeting in Spencer's on Monday, or Q Bar or whatever they call it now. Young Sutcliffe thinks they'll be coming on' train."

"Young Sutcliffe?"

"Yeah, Tony Sutcliffe's brother. He's become a bit of a big hitter while you've been away."

"Can't say I remember him."

"No, he was a just young 'un when you went down. He's looking forward to meeting you though. We'll be in there about twelve."

"Looking forward to it mate." Neil raised his glass and managed a half smile, hoping Hursty couldn't tell that he was actually dreading his first game back at Elland Road, first day back with the lads, first drink in town. Different people, different fashions, different team, different city. He'd looked forward to coming back for three years, but for some reason it just didn't feel like home anymore.

Chapter 4

Thursday 12 April 1990

Yorkshire's House Prices Settle Down – House prices in Yorkshire have remained almost static since the beginning of the year, according to a national survey, and Yorkshire house-owners are unlikely to experience the plummeting values hitting the south, says a spokesman for the Halifax Building Society. The annual house price inflation rate in the region has fallen from 24% at the end of 1989 to 15%, in marked contrast to the national average price rise of just 1% and a slump of nearly 20% in the South East. The cost of a typical semi-detached house in Leeds is now £56,300.

"Whats your favourite Stones album Reza?"

"My what?" Reza Farhad was finding it difficult to speak or breathe with Non-Stop Nigel's huge forearm tightening around his throat.

"The Rolling Stones. You can tell a lot about a man through his choice of music." Alan Connolly was eager to turn the discussion towards his favourite subject.

"Are you the sort of guy who dismisses the tracks on Emotional Rescue as unambitious and formulaic, and opts for the more obvious attractions of something like Satanic Majesties?"

"I don't understand Mr Connolly..."

"He doesn't understand Nigel." Connolly shook his head and Non-Stop Nigel lived up to his ironic nickname by maintaining his lifelong silence.

Alan Connolly stooped to retrieve a toilet brush from its holder in one of the graffiti scarred cubicles and screwed up his nose as he examined the brown tainted paper which encrusted the bristles.

"When I was a boy in Glasgow, if I dodged a question from my old man, he'd introduce me to what he called his wee friend." He slowly waved the brush under Reza's nose as the young Iranian recoiled. "And we were a big family. Always plenty of shite on our brush."

"Mmmmaybe I Can't Get No Satisfaction?"

"Maybe you can't laddie. Satisfaction wasn't the name of an album you fucking Paki halfwit." Connolly thrust the brush hard into Reza's mouth causing discoloured water to pour down his chin as he struggled under the grip of the huge man holding him.

"Keith, tell Reza what album Satisfaction was on..?" Connolly directed his question towards a rusting condom machine on the far wall and paused for an answer which no one else could hear.

"Correct brother! Satisfaction was a track on the album 'Out of our Heads' Reza. Do you think we're out of our fucking heads?" He paused from thrusting the shit-stained brush into Reza's face as the door swung open and a middle aged man in a stained tracksuit entered the toilet.

"Sorry Alan, mind if I have a quick piss?"

"Just conducting an employee briefing son. You can have a piss in the car park, no one will mind. Fuck off."

The man nervously retreated as Connolly slowly smeared the brush across Reza's contorted face, carefully positioning a papier mache wad of toilet paper on his right eyebrow.

"The fact that you're unable to name an album by the greatest fucking band in the world tells me a lot about you Reza. What do you think it tells me?"

"I don't know Mr Connolly. I don't really like music." Reza was retching as he spoke, a thick droplet of brown water suspended from his left nostril.

"Don't like music son? Don't like fucking music? What sort of person doesn't like fucking music?"

Connolly drove his fist hard into Reza's stomach twice, causing the Iranian's feet to lift involuntarily from the tiles. Non-Stop Nigel released his grip, and the sobbing youth slumped to the floor.

"The sort of person who doesn't like music is most likely the sort of person who would also have no qualms in letting his employer down. A highly untrustworthy type. You understand?"

The Cuban heel of Connolly's left boot was resting on Reza's temple and he slowly shifted his body weight onto his left leg.

"I don't know what I've done Mr Connolly." Reza grimaced as his shit stained face was pushed harder into the tiles.

"I employ you to run one of my businesses son."

"Yes, I do that. I open the café every day Mr Connolly. I keep it clean, I chase the kids out. It's doing well."

"Doing well eh? What do you think I want, a fucking Michelin star? Do I look like fucking Egon Ronay to you son?" Reza began crying loudly as the heel of Connolly's pointed black boot shifted to his cheek.

"I don't care about your fucking shitty bacon sandwiches and jacket potatoes son. Your sole aim is to run a business that deals in cash, and therefore helps provide a plausible explanation for my many and varied revenue streams. It's not hard."

"I do that Mr Connolly..."

"Aye you do. And you do it so well, I'm told you now have some regular customers."

"That's good though isn't..."

"Not when they're fucking police officers it isn't, you stupid paki cunt. Sniffing around, listening and watching. Why not just open the till and show them the takings?"

Connolly removed his foot from Reza's head and took a slow step back before delivering a toe-end just below his waistline.

"I don't care what you do, but you stop those fucking coppers coming in. Piss in the chip fat, wipe your arse on the bread, I don't care how you do it, but if I hear they're still hanging around this time next week, you'll be serving them breakfast from a fucking wheelchair. Get rid of him Nigel."

Back in the bar, Connolly shook his head as he watched Non-Stop drag Reza into the car park and deposit him in a panting heap by the bins. He then thrust a glass beneath the Jamesons optic and pushed twice.

"Doesn't like music, for fucks sake brother." He raised his glass to no one and turned to survey his domain. A fug of blue smoke hung in the light above a table of dominoes players huddled beneath the window, and an old couple sat, silently sipping halves of Tetley Mild surrounded by plastic Grandways bags. Never an audience nowadays. The side door opened and Non-Stop Nigel ducked to re-enter, followed by a stocky, dark haired man and two youths with floppy centre-parted hair.

"Fucks sake Max, what do yus think this is, St George's crypt?"

"You said you wanted to see these two boss?"

"Aye I did, but couldn't you have cleaned them up a bit first?.... Drink boys?"

With two pints of Labatts dispensed, Connolly motioned them to sit and joined them at the table.

"What's this on your shirt then, Happy Mondays? Who has a fucking happy Monday?"

"It's a band."

"A band. Some electrical synthesiser shite, no doubt. And where did you get your jeans? Did you nick them off Non-Stop here? They're about five sizes too big for yus. Fuck sake lads, you look a right state."

The two lads averted their gaze from the older man. With his leather trousers, white shirt unbuttoned to his stomach and greying, curly mullet, it would have been all too easy to refer to pots and kettles.

"Now, do I recall correctly that I recently promoted the two of yus?"

"Well you gave us a different job."

"Aye, dead right I did. Recognised your potential and elevated you within the chain of command. Management positions. Yet you still dress like a couple of fucking hippie pillheads knocking out E's in sweaty dancehalls."

The lads struggled to stifle a smirk as they continued to benefit from Connolly's life lesson.

"You have to look right for people to respect you. When my brother and me came down here in '62, we made sure we looked the part. Nice suits, proper hair styles. Isn't that right Keith?" The lads risked a nervous glance at each other during the pregnant pause which followed.

"Aye too right. We were knocking out purple hearts and black bombers in the coffee bars and at the Mecca.

Always smart though. No one would have bought off a couple of scruffy Jock cunts would they? Then we started the Mo-Mo's. Became the most feared gang in the city. Made to measure suits and no one ever dared ask us to pay. Why? Respect boys, respect. Look the part and people respect you." Connolly finished his scotch and passed his glass to Max while nodding towards the optics.

"Anyway, enough of the old chit chat. Two things. First, what's this Max tells me about you two fucking off to some dance hall on Saturday when there was business to be done?"

The lads shifted uneasily in their seats.

"It was three in the morning. We'd driven from Blackburn to Morley and dropped the gear off with the lad at Afterdark, and some lasses told us about a warehouse party near Dewsbury. There was no point going anywhere else at that time."

"So you fucked off with my gear and cash to some disco?"

"Not a disco, a rave in an industrial estate."

"And where was the stuff while you were fucking about dancing in someone's garage?"

"Hidden under the spare wheel in the boot. We were only there an hour."

"And off your fucking faces too I bet? Sampling the product...Fucks sake."

The lads looked at the floor.

"We never asked to be promoted. We were happy knocking the gear out in the clubs we'd be going to anyway."

Connolly shook his head. "Christ lads, knocking gear out in clubs. No ambition...Anyway, you like dancing do you boys?" Connolly stood and leaned across the table, whiskey breath causing them to blink.

"Max, turn the music machine on."

On a small stage in the corner of the room, lights flickered into life and a screech of feedback caused the domino players to turn, scowling. Connolly headed behind the bar and emerged clutching a silver microphone.

"If you like dancing so much lads, let's give you something to dance to."

Behind the bank of flickering lights, Connolly stooped, drink in hand, and the unmistakable scratch of stylus on vinyl filled the room, causing the doms players to jump. Connolly turned to see the lads looking confused and still in their seats.

"Nigel, help them up." The sight of the 6'7 ex-wrestler loping towards them, propelled the two youths towards the small, gum and cig-scarred dancefloor, and by the time Brian Jones sitar intro had segued into Charlie Watts staccato drum beat, it had become painfully clear what was expected. When Connolly's guttural Scottish vocals blasted through the speakers to describe seeing a red car and wanting to paint it black, they were hesitantly jerking around beneath a revolving disco ball.

"Go on boys, give it some!" urged Max, as Non-Stop Nigel patrolled the perimeter of the dance floor, silent and menacing as usual.

The doms players had resumed their game and the old couple watched impassively from behind their shopping bags, as two young men tried to recreate a Back to Basics Saturday night in a Harehills pub on a Thursday afternoon.

"Enjoy that did you?"

The lads smiled nervously and nodded as they sat down at the end of the song. Everyone in East Leeds knew that not enjoying a Stones track in the Waterloo wasn't an option unless you wanted to leave on a stretcher.

"Aye, course you did. Now, the other thing I wanted to see yus about. As you know, another important element of your new role is providing safe carriage for various items of merchandise which need transporting around the country. Newcastle tonight boys. Go with Max, he'll give you the bag. And usual drill lads – on no account do you open that fucking bag. Understand?"

Chapter 5

Saturday 14th April 1990

United Need Instant Cure -- A bad case of frayed nerves confuses fans. Leeds United are in danger of losing out on the chance of an automatic promotion spot unless they can find an instant cure for the ills which have blighted their progress in the last few matches. This was the only conclusion to draw after their disappointing showing in the defeat to Oldham which followed draws at Plymouth and at home to Bradford City and the reverse at Wolves.

"You've not told him have you?"

"I couldn't love. He'd just got out of jail. How could I tell him that?"

"So you expect me to do it? Why should I? It's your lie not mine."

"Stuart, I will love, just not yet..." Christine Yardsley sucked air into her mask and turned her eyes away from her youngest son.

"He's ringing and leaving messages on' machine mam. He wants to see me. He could turn up here now. I can't face him."

"He won't, he's working. Can't you just see him and not say owt? Nowt's changed."

"Everythings changed mam! He's not my brother..." Stuart immediately regretted raising his voice when he saw the tears forming in his mother's eyes.

"He is your brother, of course he is... He's your half brother."

"Jesus Christ. Why did I find those bloody birth certificates?" Stuart sank into an armchair, his head in his hands.

"And father unknown? What the hell does that mean? How can his father be unknown?"

"I'm not proud of it Stuart, I'm not. It was the sixties, things were different then. I was a teenager. A bloody daft teenager. His dad was Dennis Yardsley same as yours. He brought Neil up from two years old. Saying he wasn't Neil's dad is like spitting on his grave."

"I'm sorry, but just tell him mum, please. I can't look him in the eye until he knows."

"I will, in time. I promise love. What a mess eh?"

Stuart moved across the room and sat beside his mother on the sofa. She felt small and frail as he put his arm around her.

"Don't worry mam, things will get better. I've got a plan to get you out of here."

"Somewhere with a working lift would do me."

"No, somewhere much better than that. The place you've always said you wanted to go."

"Hmmm... Australia to visit your Auntie Diane. That would be nice."

"Not to visit Mum, to live. You could emigrate and live near her in Brisbane. Have a garden and a dog. Just imagine, the sun and sea air would sort your breathing out."

"Oh Stuart. You're a dreamer. How's that going to happen. Unless you've won the pools?"

Chapter 6

Monday 16th April 1990

Now United Need Nerves of Steel -- Howard Wilkinson is facing the most difficult period of his Leeds United management and his players the biggest test of character as they prepare for the crucial derby game against Sheffield United at Elland Road. A remarkable slump in fortunes over the last three weeks during which United have picked up only two points from a possible twelve, has brought intense pressure and thrown the promotion race wide open.

It was Easter Money and Neil Yardsley felt like it was his first day at junior school. The butterflies kicked in early and he was awake at 7am, pacing the bedroom and watching a gang of six year old gypsy kids trying to put a tyre over the head of a Shetland pony on Holbeck Moor.

Sixty hours graft had put nearly four hundred quid in his pocket, so he'd knocked off early on Saturday and headed into town for some clothes shopping. Hursty had told him where to go, but he'd felt like a stranger in his own city as he'd wandered around. A lot had changed in three years. The County Arcade now seemed like the place to be for the decent shops. Strand had moved down there, as had Occi, which now called itself Polo Uomo. There was a new shop called Oliver in the arcade and one in the new Schofields Centre called Ciro Citterio which Hursty had recommended, but left Neil unimpressed.

Everything in the shops seemed too bright – lots of pastel colours- greens, pinks and purples. Round neck t-shirts with patterned motifs and big logos and everything was just too baggy. He liked jeans and polo shirts to hang right, but the cut of the stuff in the shops felt wrong. The influence of musical styles from across the Pennines was obvious. Fucking Madchester.

He'd settled on a pair of Replay Jeans from Accent; some thick-soled moccasins from Moda in Pelle opposite Bond Street Centre Boots; a Timberland polo shirt from Cecil Gee and a Ralph Lauren jacket from Schofields. From observing lads around town, he felt confident his bottle-green gazelles would still pass the Elland Road fashion test. Hursty had said you'd get in nowhere after the game in trainers so it would have to be the moccasins for the match, although looking at the clumpy soles, Neil was doubtful he could run in them. Hopefully he wouldn't need to.

He'd always liked matchday mornings in town. The calm before the storm. Shift-start police mobbing up next to the station, and early out of town scarfers mooching along with wives and kids in tow, enjoying the sights of the big city on days out from small towns around the country.

Neil's pre-match ritual began with a cooked breakfast in the café opposite the Scarborough, eaten while digesting the football coverage in Sun Sport. Then up to City Square, the Black Prince pointing the way to the bookies at the back door of the station and his fixed odds coupon. It was still only eleven and he felt in need of some Dutch courage before meeting the lads, so ducked into Harlequins. Officially the bar of the adjoining Queens Hotel, the strange circular room with its high ceilings was pretty soul-less and felt like its best days were long gone. It also attracted a matchday clientele which would probably result in the loss of a star or two if hotel inspectors ever happened to call in on a Saturday lunchtime.

Neil ordered a pint of Castlemaine and handed over a pound coin only to be surprised when the barman looked back at him expectantly with his palm outstretched. He was counting the change from his £1.50 when the doors burst open behind him.

"Fuck me! Yards, you're back!" Barnsley Dave and his mates were fifteen handed and immediately transformed the previously sedate pre-lunch atmosphere. Two younger lads were with the group and Dave pushed them forward to shake hands with Neil.

"Proper lad is Yards. First lad I ever saw in a Pringle and polo neck. Train to Spurs in 81. Used to go down to London to buy your gear didn't you?"

"Used to work down there a bit so I used to pick stuff up at places like Stuarts in Shepherds Bush. They always had' Fila and Tacchini stuff before Austin Reeds and Lilywhites got it up here." It felt good to be holding court, having someone looking up to him again for the first time in years. Even better when one of Dave's mates thrust another pint into his hands.

"Neil was always trying to get one over on' plod. Tell them about Birmingham." Dave was obviously eager for some war stories and Neil was happy to oblige.

"There was a direct train from Leeds to Birmingham at ten. That was' obvious one for us to catch and we knew' law would be all over it. I spotted a connection via Manchester but kept it under wraps till 'day before the game to make sure there were no leaks. By the time' spotters arrived at' station we were already on our way to Victoria."

"Then 400 of us walked across Manchester to get the Brum train from Piccadilly. No law to be seen. The Mancs kept their heads down that morning!" Dave laughed at the memory and his young pals wished they'd been born five years earlier.

"At New Street, I told our lot to hang back when everyone piled off ' train." Neil was now holding court like a military strategist. "Twenty of us split off and walked' opposite way down' platform. Let everyone get wrapped up and escorted up towards' ground. Then we slipped out of a side door and made our own way through' backstreets. Took a few Zulus by surprise that day!"

"It was a mad day. If' Bradford Fire hadn't been' same day, I reckon they'd have kicked us and Birmingham out of ' league altogether. You did some time for that eh Yards?"

"Served a year. Sentences were always going to be harsh after' kid died. They were looking for scapegoats and unfortunately I fit the bill. Everything changed after that game. That and Bradford then Heysel straight after."

Smiles and laughter were replaced by shaken heads and solemn expressions as the far-reaching impacts of events five years earlier were recalled.

Two pints later and Neil was glad of the company of Barnsley Dave and his mates, as they headed towards Mill Hill and a reunion with the rest of the lads. A big cheer greeted their entrance to the latest reinvention of the old Black Lion, with Neil leading the group. Hursty was the first to thrust a pint towards him and the next five minutes were taken up with backslaps and handshakes from old friends.

"Surprised you aren't at Goodison mate. Or is it Anfield?" A voice from the left caused Neil to pause and turn. A kid of about twenty with dark hair, gelled into a centre parting and wearing a yellow Stone Island anorak leant on the bar, surrounded by grinning youths of a similar age.

"Sorry?" Neil became aware that the conversation around him had suddenly ceased.

"I heard you run with' scousers now mate?" The lad was smiling and stepped forward, extending his hand.

"I'm Sutcliffe. You know my older brother I think." Young Sutcliffe, the new top boy. Neil took his hand and gripped it hard, causing the younger man to smirk.

"Great to meet you Yards. I've heard a lot about you." Neil nodded, and remained silent, knowing Sutcliffe was eager for him to say the same.

"I was only joking about' scousers. You've got some mates over there though haven't you?" Aware that everyone was now listening, Neil recognised the opportunity to put the record straight, early doors.

"I was in Winson Green nick after Birmingham. All' other lads in there were Brum, Villa and Wolves. They all knew each other. I had no major problems, but they stuck to their own groups. Me and two scouse lads were' outsiders and became mates. When I got out, I was struggling for work and they put together a job and asked me if I wanted to drive. It would have been a massive payday and I couldn't turn it down. To cut a long story short, it all went tits up, ' law got tipped off and we all got nicked. Conspiracy to commit armed robbery. I got five years, served three."

"Fuck." There were sharp intakes of breath and shaken heads from the listening circle.

"That's what you get hanging round with scousers mate." Sutcliffe was laughing and Neil gripped his pint, fighting an urge to smash his forehead right into the cocky little wanker's nose.

"You back with us today then? It's gonna kick off I reckon. They're meant to be bringing a tidy firm."

"I'll believe it when I see it. They've never done owt here. I'm looking forward to' game actually. Not been for three years. Want to see this Wilko team I've been reading about."

"Massive game today mate, them bastards have been up there with us all season. I owe them one too after getting smacked in their kop when Sterland scored on Boxing Day." Hursty rubbed his nose at the memory of a painful Christmas present.

The arrival of each new group of lads into the pub resulted in more handshakes and pints thrust towards Neil but he kept an eye on the door, hoping to spot his brother.

"Any idea where our kid drinks before games Hursty? I've been back a week and still not managed to catch him."

"No idea mate. Never see him in here. It's a nice day, they might be having a pint outside Stumps. Or I've seen him a couple of times in' Boulevard. Fancy a walk up?"

"Boulevard? What's that?"

"New name for' Jubilee. They've tarted it up a bit. DJ on a Saturday night now."

"No, doesn't matter. He's obviously avoiding me for some reason. Goes to me mam's when I'm at work and doesn't return my calls."

At 2.30 the pub began to empty as fans headed to Swinegate to catch the P2's or to try to flag down a taxi.

"Christ, everyone's eager nowadays. We never used to set off until just before kick off." Neil swilled the last of his pint as Young Sutcliffe led the way to the door.

"You need to be early now mate, there'll be 34,000 there today. The good times are back!" Hursty called over his shoulder.

Neil blinked in the Spring sunlight as the group spilled out into Mill Hill, and a lad in a turquoise Benetton sweatshirt shouted and waved from the open door of an Amber Cars mini-bus outside the Prince of Wales.

"Come on, you two are with us." Neil didn't like the idea of taking orders from Young Sutcliffe, but it was a lift to the ground, so he followed the others across the road and climbed into the backseat.

The pre-match build-up on Radio Aire was crackling through the speakers, and delivering the news that Peter Haddock was out and McClelland would be starting at centre half for the first time since the 5-2 trouncing at Newcastle on the opening day of the season.

"Bad News that. Agana and Deane are going to be too quick for him." The usual Leeds pessimism was rife on the backseat, but Neil didn't care, as the van negotiated the sharp incline onto the M621 and accelerated past his mother's tower block with the Elland Road floodlights now visible in the distance.

"Off here mate, you'll get caught in traffic at' roundabout." The driver was pointed towards the Domestic Street turn and began grumbling as he joined a queue of cars at the junction.

"Straight on is best. Is moving quickly. Here is cars turning right. Making slow here always."

"Fuck off Gunga Din, you'll be out in a minute." Fifteen minutes to kick off. At least they had tickets for the Lowfields rather than the far side of the ground.

As the van picked its way along Elland Road, edging past crawling cars looking for a late parking spot, and jogging late arrivals in Top Man home shirts, Young Sutcliffe suddenly swivelled in his seat and turned to observe three lads walking on the right hand pavement.

"Blades them three. I recognise him in' Burberry jacket from' petrol station forecourt last year. Driver stop the car!"

"Oh for fucks sake, we'll miss' kick off now." Grumbling from the back seat but the seven occupants of the van were out and jogging across the road. Neil held back and paid the driver as he watched one of the suspect threesome set off running back up the road. His friends stood their ground, eyes betraying their fear, looking in vain for an escape route.

"Where you from lads?"

"Penistone. We're Leeds..." One of the lads had only just started with his dubious alibi when Young Sutcliffe's fist landed on his temple, knocking him sideways. His friend turned to run but was felled by a well-aimed Rockport shoe to the shins. He curled into a foetal ball beneath a volley of kicks and stamps. The first lad had bounced off the steel railed fence bordering the M621 and was crouching beneath a rapid succession of blows to the back of the head. A knee to the face sent him crashing forward to the ground and his beige Burberry jacket disappeared beneath a stampede of brown shoes and blue trainers.

Young Sutcliffe was too engrossed in delivering a flurry of machine-like punches to the back of the lad's head to notice Neil approaching. He seemed surprised as Neil's arms enveloped him in a bear hug and pulled him away from his victim.

"What the fuck...?"

"Leave them."

"They're fucking blades you wanker. I recognise them."

"So what, there's two of them and eight of us. It's not on." The rest of the lads had ceased their attack and the Sheffield fans staggered to their feet. One jogged blindly into the road, narrowly missing being hit by a passing black and white taxi.

"Fuck off lads. You got lucky." Neil pointed them down the road towards the ground.

"What's the matter with you? Do you think they'd have given two of us a free pass at Bramall Lane?"

"If it was their proper lads, yes I do. If it was a bunch of chavvy little cunts, probably not." Neil dropped his arms by his side and clenched his fists as Young Sutcliffe approached.

"Fucking hell..." Sutcliffe stopped his advance, sniffed and spat.

"Come on, we're gonna miss' kick off now." His shoulder brushed Neil as he passed and the rest of the group turned and followed him down Elland Road.

The game was already ten minutes old when they filed through the rusting turnstiles of the Lowfields Road stand and Neil felt the familiar rush of excitement as they headed up the uncovered stairs towards the seats. At the top of the steps they were met by a line of police officers who blocked their way, with batons drawn.

"Down that way lads, you can't come this side."

"Our seats are that way." Young Sutcliffe brandished his ticket towards a steward in a Showsec anorak.

"Well you'll have to go round. You can't come this way." A sergeant in a blue riot helmet shoved Sutcliffe in the chest.

"Sheff United are in here." A Leeds fan in an Aquascutum cap on the back row of the seats turned and nodded towards the right hand side of the stand. "They got sussed straight away. About thirty of them. Police have got them surrounded."

"Bollocks. I told you they were turning up." Young Sutcliffe shook his head at a chance missed.

"Looks like standards have slipped while I was away. No one would ever get away with that a few years back." Neil smirked, unable to resist having a dig at his young rival.

They took their seats with Sutcliffe and his mates remaining standing to pick out the Blades group on the back two rows.

"That fucking Rowley's there. He's their top lad. We'll try to get up to them at half time."

Neil shook his head. A few years earlier he'd have been with them, leading from the front. Now he was just happy to be back at Elland Road, watching a game.

The atmosphere was tense, with Leeds faltering in their promotion charge, having dropped ten points in the last four games. Early pressure from the home side quickly paid off and within five minutes of Neil and his mates arriving in the ground, they were celebrating the first goal as Strachan poked home a rebound from a Kamara shot in front of a packed South Stand terrace. With half time approaching, Young Sutcliffe rose from his seat.

"Come on, let's go for a wander." The rest of the lads stood up, but Neil remained in his seat.

"You not coming?" Sutcliffe nudged Neil's legs as he passed.

"No. I'm watching the match. I've not been for three years and I've already missed most of ' first half because of you, fucking about." Sutcliffe brushed past and muttered something Neil didn't catch.

"Get us a pie." Neil winked as Hursty set off up the terrace steps and his mate smiled back.

They returned as the second half began, and Young Sutcliffe was drawing everyone's attention to a large swelling above his right eye.

"Copper blindsided me!" he directed his comments to no-one in particular but made sure Neil could hear. "We'll have another go at the end of the game."

The match remained evenly balanced until fifteen minutes from the end when the youngster Gary Speed hared down the left wing and crossed for Lee Chapman to tap home from the edge of the six yard box. The two goal cushion settled the nerves and Leeds began to enjoy themselves, attacking the kop end. Wilkinson had directed his strikers to stand in front of the Sheffield keeper, Simon Tracey, to prevent his long kicks upfield. Bobby Davison followed the instruction to the letter and repeatedly frustrated the keeper as he tried to kick the ball out. As the match approached the final ten minutes, Davison charged down an attempted clearance and the Blades player dragged him to the ground. Strachan floated the penalty into the top corner. All that remained was for Speed to break from a Sheffield corner and leave everyone trailing in his wake as he sprinted towards Tracey's goal to 'get one yourself son.' 4-0 against their main promotion rival on a sunny April afternoon was about as good as it had got for Leeds in recent years, and the fans were jubilant as they streamed away from the ground. 'When we win promotion, this is what we'll sing...' now seemed more like a prediction rather than a hopeful dream.

The police surrounded the Blades fans in the top corner of the stand and Young Sutcliffe marshalled his troops to plan how to breach the security cordon. Neil just wanted to relive the game over a few pints.

"Fancy a walk up to' White Hart and' Whistlestop Hursty?"

"Yeah go on then. Nowt will happen down here."

Walking up Wesley Street, it felt good to be out for a post-match drink again with his best mate. Neil had met Hursty on his first day at Matthew Murray in 1979. Starting a new school in the 4th form when all the other kids already knew each other wasn't easy. He'd wanted to stay at St Michaels when they moved from Saxton Gardens to Beeston, but his mum was having none of it. It had added to the tension between them, caused by her starting a new relationship within a year of his dad dying. And then they'd had to move from East Leeds to this bloke Martin's house in Beeston, filled with furniture and knick-knacks from his first marriage. Neil would inherit Martin's grown-up daughter's old bedroom, while Stuart got a small box room overlooking the backyard.

Predictably, on his first day at school south of the river, the new kid had been singled out for some unwanted attention in the dinner queue, and a 5th form skinhead called Cunningham had homed in on the badges on Neil's Harrington.

The Specials weren't even Neil's favourite band, but he knew he couldn't simply let Cunningham remove the small plastic circle with the 2-Tone logo from his jacket. He'd waited till the skinhead's fat fingers were fumbling to undo the safety pin, before knocking him sideways with a fierce right uppercut. When Cunningham had got to his feet he'd faced a gang of 4th year boys, led by Hursty, lining up behind Neil.

"Cunningham's a wanker. Used to wear a denim jacket with Hawkwind and Led Zep patches till last year," Hursty had laughed.

He and Neil soon became best mates, graduating from 2-Tone, Fred Perry and Harringtons to striped boating blazers, black and white 'Jam' shoes and fishtail parkas. Both regulars at Elland Road, they were eating chips outside United Fisheries one October Saturday in 1980 when they'd watched a scuffle develop between some older lads. One group were Leeds fans, wearing the standard terrace uniform of docs and donkey jackets. The others were Everton fans, but they didn't look like any sort of football fan Neil and Hursty had ever seen before. They wore straight leg cords in burgundy; strange white trainers with straps instead of laces; polo neck sweaters and cardigans. Their hair was cut into a fringe like Joanna Lumley's Purdey character in the New Avengers.

"Who are these puffs?" Hursty had wondered aloud, until one of the scousers had flashed the sort of knife that Neil's dad had used for cutting carpets, and sent the Leeds fans back-pedalling. Within weeks, the same look started appearing on the Lowfields terrace at Elland Road and soon Neil and Hursty were cultivating their own 'flickhead' haircuts, and wearing golf jumpers shoplifted from Lilywhites to go drinking underage at the Precinct or Gemini on a Friday night.

After Leeds relegation in 1982, Elland Road had become a depressing place, as crowds fell to below 15,000 and a team of has-beens and journeymen struggled against the likes of Cambridge and Shrewsbury. Away days were always lively though, and a match against Leeds guaranteed a turn-out of every psycho and violent offender living in small towns across the country. Avoiding the heavily policed football special trains, Neil, Hursty and thousands of teenagers like them criss-crossed the country every weekend, living on their wits, trying to avoid getting a kicking or an arrest, and forging friendships which would last a lifetime.

Then in 85 it had all gone wrong. TV footage of Millwall's Bushwackers chasing Bedfordshire police across Luton's pitch; the young lad dying at Birmingham; the Bradford fire; and then Heysel, had placed football's decaying stadia and unruly supporters firmly in the sights of Margaret Thatcher's Government. The Popplewell inquiry would lead to the introduction of all-seater grounds, and police budgets would be increased to root out troublemakers. Much tougher sentences would be handed out to offenders. Offenders like Neil Yardsley.

"Brighton on Saturday. I can get us in a tranny van if you fancy it?" Hursty was still buzzing after the victory, as they stood at the bar in the Whistlestop. Five years ago, Neil would have been up for it, but at the age of 25 and after spending four of the last five years in a confined space, eight hours bouncing around the cold steel floor of a van held little appeal.

"I might have gone if we could have clinched promotion, but think I'll give it a miss, thanks."

"Save it for Bournemouth eh?"

Neil was about to ask about plans for the final game of the season, when the pub door burst open and a youth in a mustard coloured hoody fell into the bar. There was blood beneath his nose and a large rip down the front of his top.

"They're here...! Outside now. Minibus!"

There was a split second of silence as everyone in the pub turned to face the door, followed by a cry of 'Goooon Leeds!' as stools were upturned and bottles and pint glasses grabbed in a rush towards the exit.

A booming chant of 'Leeds! Leeds! Leeds!' rang out as the room emptied towards the car park. Hursty was on his way out of the door and turned to see his friend still standing at the bar.

"You not coming?"

"Can't risk it mate." Neil took a gulp of his pint and watched as floppy-haired lads in baggy jeans vaulted the small fence surrounding the pub before jogging unsteadily down the road.

"You do right love. Not worth the bother." The barmaid lit a cigarette and poured herself a half, as a flashing blue light passed the window.

Ten minutes later the door flew open and the first of dozens of breathless, red-faced men entered, gesticulating and talking loudly. They were quickly followed by a similar number of black-clad police in riot gear, some struggling to restrain slavering Alsatians on short leads. The sound of frenzied barking drowned out the Home and Away theme tune from a TV in the corner. Hursty appeared at Neil's side, as the police began to identify targets and handcuff them.

"Jesus, it went right off then. All the windows in their mini-bus have gone through."

Through the crowd, Neil made eye contact with a familiar face, who smiled and elbowed his way towards him.

"Oh shit, look who's here."

"Now then Mr Yardsley, I didn't realise you were out." The equine face of the Leeds police 'spotter' Andy Barton peered from beneath the visor of his helmet.

"Got out last week."

"And already back in trouble. Fuck me lad, you must love it inside."

"I haven't done owt. I was here the whole time." Neil looked to the barmaid for confirmation and she nodded.

"He was love, he's been stood here all along."

"Well, we'll soon find out, because we caught the whole thing on video from the hoolivan. So until we know one way or the other...you're nicked. Both of you." Barton nodded towards Hursty and Neil, and uniformed officers turned them round to face the bar. Within a week of being released, Neil Yardsley was back in handcuffs.

Chapter 7

Tuesday 17th April 1990

Black Rule 'Not the Answer' – President FW de Klerk has again rejected black rule in South Africa, but said apartheid must end. At the start of a four day parliamentary debate, he promised to create 'a new and just South Africa' but had no word on new measures to dismantle 42 years of apartheid. Instead he demanded an 'unequivocal commitment' from Nelson Mandela's African National Congress to give up violence in its struggle against white rule.

The gas bill was brown and stiff as Julie Statham peeled it from the radiator. The British Telecom logo in the corner of the phone bill was barely visible through a layer of dried coffee stain. The red mortgage arrears letter had turned a shade of purple when Marmaduke the cat had sent a full mug of Nescafe spilling across the table as she'd conducted her daily cash juggling exercise.

She stared out of the window to the neatly trimmed lawn and circle of identical Wimpey semis in the quiet cul-de-sac. Some dwarf conifers would look nice along the edge of the lawn. Once they got out of this mess, she imagined dragging Richard along to Texas or Homebase, and emerging with a trolley full of greenery. Once they got out of this mess. If they got out of it. The move to Garforth had stretched them financially and then Richard had lost his job at just the wrong time. All a terrible misunderstanding, but he'd had to resign. All that was behind them now. He'd gone self-employed and seemed back on track. Working late as usual.

The sound of a car turning into the cul-de-sac interrupted Julie's daydreams and she stood to see her husband swing the Sierra into the driveway in a flamboyant arc. She shooed Marmaduke from the kitchen doorway with a slippered foot and bent to light the oven.

Richard was stooping to retrieve something from his briefcase when she entered the room.

"Hiya love, good day?"

He turned away momentarily, then turned back to face her, both arms behind his back.

"Very good day!" He smiled. "I've got a surprise."

The cash appeared with a flourish, spreading across the table of unpaid bills and fluttering to the carpet in a cascade of red and purple.

"My god. What...where's that come from Richard?"

"A gift." He smiled and slumped onto the couch.

Julie remained facing the table. She didn't want to look at him. She urged herself to remain calm but could feel the panic welling up inside her and the prickle of tears in the corners of her eyes.

"750 quid. That should clear most of the utilities bills and a month of mortgage..."

"For God's sake Richard...!" Julie couldn't hold her emotions any longer and dashed into the kitchen to turn the oven down.

"What? What's the matter?"

"It's happening again isn't it?

"What is? What's happening?"

"Gambling! You're fucking gambling again!" The tears poured down Julie's cheeks and she could feel a nervous rash spreading from her chest, up her throat towards her face.

"No. No. It's a bonus. A gift from a client."

"You're lying, I know when you're lying. What did you win it on?"

"I helped a guy save a lot of money on his tax return and he said he wanted to give me a bonus, that's all. Why do you always think the worst?"

"Because it always is the worst. How many times does this have to happen for you to realise? You need help Richard."

"I can't do right for doing fucking wrong in this house." Richard picked up his jacket and headed towards the front door. The house shook as he slammed it closed and left Julie Statham on her hands and knees, picking up coffee stained red bills and tear stained bank notes.

Chapter 8

Thursday 19th April 1990

Stamp out 'Acid House' Parties – New measures are being urged to stop the spread of so called 'Acid House' parties in Yorkshire. York City Council is being pressed by its officers to act swiftly to prevent the gatherings, which attract up to 20,000 people and which are a fertile market for drug dealers. The parties are organised at a secret location with thousands of young people flocking to them. Now York's environmental health chiefs have put forward a series of measures to stop such parties being held in the city.

"What a bloody mess Julie. What am I going to do?" Christine Yardsley sucked air from her mask and tilted her head away from a shaft of sunlight breaching the gloom of the room.

"I was so stupid. I forgot all about Neil's birth certificate and when Stuart needed his to apply for a passport, I just told him where they were. There it was in black and white. Neil Harrison, boy, father unknown. Mother Christine Harrison, 19."

Julie emerged from the kitchen with two cups of tea.

"It must have been hard for you back then. How long was it till you met your husband?"

"I met Dennis in 1966, the year after Neil was born. Imagine, taking on a girl with a year old baby, but he never minded. We got married in 69 and he raised Neil as his own, so when Neil started school I called him Yardsley. He never knew any different. Stuart was born in 1970 and they looked so alike. No one would ever have guessed they weren't full brothers."

"So what happened to Neil's real father?"

Christine closed her eyes and shook her head, unable to look Julie in the eye.

It was clear she didn't feel able to answer so Julie broke the awkward silence which had descended. "You really should tell him now that Stuart knows. It will be hard, but I think it's best in the long run."

"He's just come back Julie. I don't want to drive him away again."

"He's a grown man now. He's old enough to know the truth."

Christine sipped at her tea and the room fell silent again.

"How are you anyway love? You look tired. Have they got you working double shifts again?"

"I don't mind to be honest. We need the money." Julie sighed and stared at the three bars of the gas fire.

"Everything alright with you and...?"

"Richard."

"Richard. That's right. Is everything okay?" Before Christine had got the final word out Julie's face had crumpled and she'd begun to cry.

"Oh love, I'm sorry...what's the matter? You don't have to say though...it's none of my business."

"I don't mind telling you. I've no one else to talk to since my mum died. I can trust you..."

"Of course you can. I don't bloody see anyone to tell even if I wanted to." Christine smiled behind her mask and Julie laughed through her sobs.

"We're up to our eyes in debt. Richard lost his job just after we bought the new house and the bills just piled up."

"That's bad luck love, it really is..."

"It's not bad luck though. It's his fault. He gambles. Casinos, horses, football you name it. He's lost a fortune of our money."

"Oh I'm sorry Julie, I had no idea."

"He says he's stopped but he walked in the other night and handed me a load of cash. Came up with some unbelievable story about where it came from. I know though. It's happening again."

Silence again as Christine struggled to find a silver lining to Julie's cloud.

"Then we had a row, and he went out last night and never came back. He comes and goes at all hours. I don't even know where he's working or what he's doing. He's become so secretive. I think he might be having an affair."

"No I'm sure that's not right love. A lovely wife like you...why would he? Anyway, I've no room to talk about secrets have I?" Christine smiled softly.

"I suppose not. But just think, once you've told Neil that's it. It's done. No more secrets."

Christine took a deep gulp from her mask.

"Julie....the birth certificate isn't right. I do know who Neil's dad was."

Chapter 9

Monday 23rd April 1990

Poll Tax Papers up in Smoke -- Scores of poll tax books went up in smoke in a demonstration against the community charge in Leeds. About 50 members of 'Beeston against the Poll Tax' gathered at Cross Flatts park on Saturday to burn their payment books in an act of defiance.

"Thank God for that, he's stopped." Bob McGinn slapped his domino on the table with a crack, the way the old Jamaicans did it in the Fforde Grene. The rest of the table chuckled through the fog of roll-up smoke, but then stopped abruptly as they looked over Bob's shoulder.

Bob turned to see Connolly striding over from the stage, dressed as usual like a low-rent Tom Jones, in tight leather trousers and a white shirt with a big collar, his face like thunder and muttering angrily to himself.

"Do any of you boys still have a wife?"

They shuffled uneasily on their stools.

"I do Alan. You know Marie..." Little Malcolm was the first to break the silence.

"Aye Marie. Lovely girl. You and her ever get romantic Mal?"

"Erm...not sure what you mean Alan. We've been wed forty years..."

"Hmmm. Tell me this Mal. Imagine if yus went home from here one night and Marie opened the door in the old frilly nightie. She's done her hair and make-up, got the old stockings and suspenders on. You know what I'm saying?" Connolly had taken up position behind the hunched figure of Bob McGinn who was cowering on his stool. Little Malcolm squirmed as his friends laughed nervously.

"I doubt that would happen Alan. As I said, we've been married forty years..."

"But just imagine..." Connolly rested his hands on McGinn's shoulders and squeezed gently. Bob felt a chill run down his spine.

"Imagine, yus come home, and she's there in the stockings and sussies, with her lips all red and pouting. Maybe she's got the old high heels out of the wardrobe. You get me Mal?"

"I-I- think so, but I don't think...'

"And yus come through that fucking door, walk straight past her and put the telly on, ignoring the obvious attraction of her charms...how do you think she's going to feel?"

"Well..."

"I'll tell you how she's going to feel. She'll be fucking furious! That's how she'll feel." Connolly's hands were now gently caressing Bob McGinn's balding head, and he could feel cold beads of sweat starting to appear on his neck.

"Your poor Marie has gone out of her way to provide for your enjoyment, and you've rejected it Mal. She didn't have to do that for yus, but she took the time and trouble to do so, and you didn't even look at her. She has every right to be furious. Isn't that right brother?"

Connolly's voice had dropped to a slow whisper and his fingers gently ruffled Bob's comb-over into a floppy mohawk. Connolly nodded his head in response to an answer only he could hear.

"Do yus know where I'm going with this wee analogy boys?"

No one spoke. The klaxon tune of an ice cream van tinkled in the distance and five cigarettes burnt dangerously close to fingers suspended in front of lined faces.

"Bob... Robert. Where do yus think I'm heading with this hypothetical situation?" Connolly bent to whisper in Bob McGinn's ear as his fingers slowly tapped on the top of the old man's head. Bob gulped and he was unable to find any saliva in his mouth.

"Singing?" he croaked

"What was that Bob?" Connolly's fetid breath tickled his cheek.

"You were singing along to the Stones and we..."

"You what Bob?"

"We weren't...erm, paying full attention."

"Full attention eh? Not paying full attention was it?"

"Maybe...we were just concentrating on..."

"You weren't paying ANY attention you ungrateful fucking cunts!"

Connolly clapped his hands hard on the sides of Bob McGinn's head and Bob felt his ear drums explode.

"Sympathy for the Devil. six minutes, eighteen fucking seconds of complex lyrics and subtle hidden meanings. A lyrically perfect performance delivered from memory , and you...you fucking ungrateful wee bastards sit there tapping your doms on your table without even turning around. Let alone any applause!"

Two examiners from the driving test centre who had been sat at the bar headed quickly out of the side door and almost collided with Non-Stop Nigel and Max coming the other way.

"Gaffer?"

Connolly had raised his finger towards the cowering table of elderly men and seemed to be considering their punishment when he was distracted.

"Can we have a word?"

Connolly turned back to the table.

"You ungrateful wee bastards! Next time you WILL fucking clap."

Alan Connolly shook his head as he strode behind the bar and tapped the Jamesons optic twice with his glass.

"Right Max, what's going on?"

"The bag for the Dutchman is ready. Who's doing the drop?"

"Give it to the pillheads..."

"Danno and Stuart...?"

"I don't know their fucking names. Those scruffy little cunts in the baggy clothes." Connolly swigged off his drink and poured another double.

"You sure you want them to go boss? Not me and Nigel?"

"Aye. Get them on it. I need you boys to track down that fucking accountant."

"We keep missing him. He's been doing the pick-ups though so he's around. We're leaving messages but he's not getting back to us. The address he gave us is a boarded up shop unit."

Connolly stood up, drink in hand and smiled at no one, then leant behind the bar and retrieved a silver bladed bayonet with a wooden handle.

"They're all at it brother. Fucking robbing us blind, just like you said they would."

Max and Non-Stop Nigel exchanged worried glances. Six months earlier, Connolly's conversations with his long dead brother had become less frequent, following a consultation with a new psychiatrist and an amended prescription. Now, after announcing that he could see things with a new clarity, Connolly had dispensed with his tablets and Keith Connolly, deceased, was once again calling the shots.

"Aye, you're right there brother. Think they can stitch us up because we're a couple of wee Scottish boys. Just two wee Glasgow lads against the world now. Take no prisoners eh..!" Connolly laughed and ran his finger along the bayonet's blade.

"So, the boys get the bag and we go look for the accountant boss?" Max and Nigel stood, awaiting their boss's orders.

"Aye Maxie. My numbers are down again and that bastard's going to need a fucking good explanation this time, or he'll wish he never got his maths 'O' level. You go find him and bring him back for a visit with uncle Alan."

Alan Connolly tilted the bayonet and admired the glint of the blade under the bar light, a malevolent smile forming as he imagined the silver turning red as it opened the accountants throat.

"No prisoners brother. No fucking prisoners."

Chapter 10

Wednesday 25 April 1990

The Battle of Strangeways-- More than 100 prison officers in riot gear stormed Strangeways jail, regaining control of the main buildings, but only one of the last six rioters was arrested in the early stages of the assault, which began the 25th day of the siege.

We Can Handle the Pressure -- Sterland's Promotion Pledge- Leeds United, now within striking distance of a return to the 1st division were in unrelenting mood today, as they put the finishing touches to their preparation for what promises to be a tricky derby against Barnsley at Elland Road (7.30) tonight. Suggestions that Howard Wilkinson's side have hit a late 'wobble' were brushed aside as fullback Mel Sterland mirrored the feeling of his teammates when he said today "We have come too far along the road now to blow it in the final stages."

The thumping electro beat of Lil Louis' French Kiss, 12' mix did little to lift the mood in Stuart and Danno's small kitchen.

The holdall sat in the centre of the table, next to an overflowing ashtray, a bean-stained plate, three empty Stella cans and a Grolsch bottle turned into a candle holder. The bag was sky blue with a leaping puma and the word Slazenger in navy.

Stuart and Danno stared at it, as they had been doing since Max had delivered it that morning, with instructions that this was an important delivery. No room for error or fucking about going to raves this time.

"I keep expecting the door to get kicked in." Danno was chewing on his nails and twitching involuntarily. "It's either a lot of gear or guns, it's got to be."

"If it's guns, there can't be many. It's not that heavy." Stuart leant forward and flicked at the zip.

"You haven't picked it up have you?"

"Yeah. Just to feel the weight. We're going to have to pick it up to get it to the car aren't we?"

"It fucking scares me shitless Stu. I wish we'd never got into this. How did knocking out a few pills in clubs turn into being couriers for gangsters. This is bad, I can feel it..."

"I'm going to open it." Stuart stood up.

"Fuck off! I don't want to be anywhere near if you do that. What if they know?"

"How will they know?"

" I don't know. What if there's an alarm?

"How's Connolly going to hear it when he's in Harehills and we're in Headingley?"

"I don't know, but what if there's a transmitter or summat? I could tell by the way Max said it, if they find we've opened it, they'll kill us. And probably torture us first."

Stuart took a deep breath and leant towards the bag like a bomb disposal expert approaching a ticking mechanism. Danno retreated to the corner of the room where he crouched with his hands over his face.

Stuart gently tugged open the zip, pulled the bag open and peered inside.

Danno peered from between his fingers.

"What is it Stu?"

Stuart turned to face his friend. "Weed. It's a big bag of weed that's all. Tonight we go to the Barnsley game, then first thing tomorrow drive to Hull and drop it off. Job done. No problem."

Danno remained on the floor, shaking his head. "I just want to see the back of it. And I want to get out of this whole fucking mess. I want my old life back."

Chapter 11

Neil dumped the van outside his mum's flats and set off jogging across Holbeck Moor. 7pm. Half an hour to kick off, so still time for a couple of quick pints. Through the tunnel and across Domestic street, seeing the mob of lads drinking outside the Waggon as soon as he turned the corner by the kebab shop.

"Bar's a nightmare, you might as well get some cans from' offy." Hursty shouted as he approached. "Get me a couple of bottles of Bud."

"Heard you got lifted against Sheff United, even though you did nowt." Young Sutcliffe, grinning in his face and emphasising 'did nowt' as he crossed the road from the corner shop, but Neil refused to rise to the bait.

"Well at least I'm not waiting for the 6 o'clock knock now. They've got it all on video and that will show I wasn't even there."

"Yeah, I heard your arse went again." Sutcliffe's mates grinned and sniggered like the naughty kids they were, taking the piss out of the grown-ups.

"Bad result Saturday. Dropped two points there." Neil couldn't be bothered getting into it with the little prick and turned to Hursty. "Blades are only one point behind us now, Geordies three. Barnsley need the points tonight too, they could still go down."

"Yeah but they're shite. No problem tonight. Haddock's back too I think."

"Barnsley will bring fuck all tonight. Fancy themselves at home but they won't travel..." Young

Sutcliffe was providing an off-field prediction for his mates.

"Jesus, you're one boring fucker aren't you kid? Forget it. It's over, you're five years too late." Neil swigged off the dregs of his bottle and tossed it onto the scrubby grass verge.

"South Stand tonight Hursty?" He turned away before Sutcliffe had a chance to respond.

"Aye, come on let's get down there."

Sitting in the Lowfields for the Sheffield game had added to the strangeness of Neil's Elland Road homecoming, but the Barnsley game felt more like old times. He'd always preferred the South Stand to the Kop, right back to the early 80's when the lads had relocated to the seats there. Back then it was closer to the away fans, and standing with the great unwashed at the back of the Gelderd wasn't the best idea when you were wearing white trainers, bleached jeans and eighty quid tracksuit tops. Now the South Stand was back to being terracing and Neil didn't mind how packed it was.

Again, the old stadium seemed to be electrified with a nervous energy and as the teams took the field beneath the most ostentatious floodlights in football, Neil was transported back to big nights like this from his childhood, seeing Bremner's Leeds tackle Cruyff's Barcelona as a ten year old.

Leeds attacked the South Stand in the first half and should have had a penalty when Sterland was clipped in the box. They piled on the pressure but the score remained level until Chris Fairclough rose to head the ball home right in front of Neil and Hursty just before half time. The terraces erupted around them and they were transported down ten steps in a jubilant surge of emotion and relief.

Half time was a chance for Hursty to borrow a programme from the lad next to him to work out the permutations for the remaining games. It was tight at the top, and it was looking more and more likely that the outcome of the season would go right to the wire, and Leeds final game at Bournemouth.

As the teams lined up for the second half kick off, Neil turned and started to head up the terrace.

"Where you off to?"

"For a piss. Told you before, my dad always taught us this is the best time to go to the bog to avoid the queues."

Heading down the steps to the concourse, dodging fans coming the other way juggling coffee, soup and Wagon Wheels, Neil spotted a familiar gait brushing through the crowd and heading into the toilet.

There were spaces at the silver trough urinals now, but Neil waited until a man in a flat cap and anorak moved away, then took his place alongside the youth in the green hooded top.

"You avoiding me then?"

"Fucks sake...Neil. I was miles away then. Nearly shit meself!"

"So I don't even get a welcome home then? Thought we'd have been for a pint by now..."

Stuart puffed out his cheeks as he buttoned his fly.

"I've been busy mate."

"So I've heard. What happened to the painting job with Dougie?"

"Don't start Neil..." Stuart turned and walked to the sink with its ever-running cold tap.

"I will fucking start! I'm locked up and I'm hearing you've become some sort of big time, fucking gangster drug dealer..."

"How am I a gangster then? You don't know a fucking thing..."

"Well you tell me then...I hear you jacked your job in to drive round selling gear in clubs. That you're taking all sorts of that shit yourself, then that you're some sort of errand boy for Alan Connolly..."

Stuart turned towards his brother then looked at the puddled floor of the toilet. The ceiling shook to the sound of a roar as Leeds were denied another penalty.

"Well?"

"It's none of your business Neil."

"It IS my fucking business!" Neil punched a cubicle door in frustration. "You were just a kid when dad died, you don't remember. I was twelve. I'll always remember..."

"Yeah yeah, I know, in the hospital, he said you're the man of the house now, you have to look after Mum and Stu. I've heard it all before Neil, and it's all bollocks."

"It's true."

"So what if it is? You've been in' nick for most of the last five years. I've had to watch mum slowly dying in that shitty flat. What the fuck have you done to look after her? Answer...not a fucking thing."

Neil breathed heavily as a loud groan from above signified another Leeds miss.

"I'm back now..."

"Yeah you're back. Running round with your fucking hooligan mates again. I heard you got nicked against Sheff United. You'll be back inside in a month or so."

"No, I didn't, I won't...It's different now. Things have changed."

"Look, our kid. I don't want to argue with you, but you haven't been here. I've had to do things I didn't want to do. I'm going to sort things for Mum. See you around eh?"

Stuart turned and shoved open the toilet door with his foot and headed up the steps to the terrace with Neil jogging to keep up.

"Are you going to follow me around all night?"

There was no route through the tightly packed bodies on the terrace, so Stuart squeezed into a space on the top step, with his brother alongside him.

"I just want to know what's going on Stu. That Connolly is bad news. A proper nutter. I've fucked my life up, I don't want you doing the same."

"I'm not daft Neil....go on Mel, go past him...ah for fuck's sake."

"You are daft though. If you get done working for him it won't be a couple of years, you'll be looking at life."

"I won't be working for him much longer... Go on Bobby, knock it past him...pah, Davisons legs have gone in this game."

"Just level with me Stu. I don't want to fight with you."

Stuart took a step forwards so he was now looking up at his brother.

"Okay." He nodded back towards the concourse and Neil followed him down seven steps to the middle of the stairway.

"I'm going to get mum out of the flat. Going to pay her way to Australia, set her up in a flat there near Auntie Diane, near the beach." Stuart's eyes flicked nervously down the stairs as he recounted his plan.

Neil stared at his brother, then began to speak, but his words were lost in the deafening noise from the terrace. *'We are Leeds, we are Leeds, we are Leeds.'*

"Just listen. After tonight, you won't see me again for a while, but I'll be in touch when things are in place, and you can sort things this end. Okay?"

"What the fuck are you talking about Stu?"

"In my flat now, there's a bag. Tomorrow morning, me and Danno have to take it to Hull and drop it off with a bloke at a garage. But that's not going to happen. Instead it will be coming with me on the first train to London."

Neil was smiling and shaking his head as the tannoy announced a Barnsley substitution- Brendan O'Connell replacing Paul Futcher.

"And what's in this bag then?"

"Cash. About 25 grand I reckon. Danno thinks it's weed. The less he knows the better."

"Are you absolutely fucking crackers?"

"No. I've thought it all through. I can stay with Skinner from school, he lives in Camden now. There's loads of travel agents in London who deal with Oz flights and property rentals. I've applied for a visa for Mam and once it's all arranged I'll let you know and you can explain it to her and sort things this end."

"They'll kill you Stu. No messing about, they'll torture you and chop you up. You'll just disappear. It's what they do."

"They'd better not find me then had they?"

A gasp, a collective groan and distant celebrations from 600 South Yorkshire voices indicated that Barnsley had equalised. Stuart headed back up to the terrace as Neil sat on the steps and stared into the strip-lit gloom of the South Stand concourse. His brother was about to make a life changing, life threatening mistake, and he couldn't escape the feeling that it was all his fault. 'Look after your mum and Stuart' had been his father's last words to him, yet he'd failed them both, and broken his promise. He rejoined his brother on the top step as Barnsley gained a throw-in by the West Stand corner flag.

"You can't do it Stu, I won't let you."

"You won't let me? I'm not a kid anymore Neil, you don't own me, you don't control me."

A long throw, four step run-up, looping at speed towards the Leeds six-yard-box.

"I made a promise to look after you, to our dad, on his deathbed."

A Barnsley head, first to the ball, flicked across the box.

"He's not your dad," whispered, unheard.

White shirt closest, blue shirt rushing in.

"What did you say?"

"I said he wasn't your fucking Dad, Neil. I'm sorry."

Owen Archdeacon at the far post, ball in the Leeds net.

"Ask Mum. I'm sorry."

Stuart put his head down and ducked into the crowd, disappearing into a sea of disbelief and anguish.

Leeds were falling apart again.

Chapter 12

Christine Yardsley had been tucked up in bed reading hew new Catherine Cookson novel when Neil had come bursting into her room, breathless having run a mile from Elland Road.

"What is it love? What's up?" Neil didn't reply and stood panting in the doorway, shaking his head.

"You're scaring me Neil, what is it?"

"I saw Stu at the match..."

The expression on Neil's face stopped Christine from coming out with the expected pleasantries over her sons' reunion. She looked down at her book, knowing what was coming.

"He told me that dad isn't my real dad mam..."

The page blurred as tears formed in her eyes and she felt her chest tighten.

"He's lying isn't he? Why would he say that mam? Why would he say it?"

Christine gasped and reached for her mask. She still couldn't look at her son, standing in her bedroom doorway, breathless and now sobbing like a little boy. Her silence told him the answer.

"Oh mam no. It's true isn't it?"

Christine continued to stare, unseeing, at her book as Neil's raised voice cracked as he spoke.

" Why? Why mam? Twenty five years. You've lied to me for the whole of my life."

Christine gulped air and shook her head, meeting Neil's imploring eyes for the first time. 'I'm sorry' was all she could think to say, but the words wouldn't come and instead the only sound was the hiss of oxygen filling the mask.

She wanted him to punish her. Shout and scream, throw things around the room, call her a disgrace, a bad mother, a whore, a liar. And then collapse in tears on the bed where she could comfort him. Tell him she was sorry. That not a day had gone by when she wished she hadn't started the lie she'd lived with for more than half her life.

But he didn't. 'How could you?' was all he asked before leaving the room. Leaving Christine Yardsley lying in her bed, listening to her son crying through the wall, her own tears soaking the paperback she clutched in shaking hands, while gasping at the air through her mask.

Chapter 13

Thursday 26 April 1990

Cancer boy jets out to see Michael Jackson -- A 13 year old Wakefield boy dying of a rare form of cancer, is to have a dream come true when he meets pop superstar Michael Jackson in Los Angeles. Jason Rudger who has been fighting cancer for four years has now been told his condition, affecting both lungs, is inoperable.

United's Night of Agony -- Performances like this should carry a health warning. Leeds United would be well advised to post warning notices to the effect that watching Howard Wilkinson's men in action just now might seriously damage your health.

"You okay gaffer?"

Max had worked for Alan Connolly long enough to know that a full ash tray, a glass of scotch on the bar and the melancholy refrain of 'Angie' booming from the Waterloo's speakers at 11am were all signs that things weren't going well.

"Have you found him?" Connolly's voice boomed from the speaker. Max tapped an imaginary microphone to remind his boss that his voice could be heard across the street.

"Eh? What? Have you found that thieving fucking bastard accountant?"

Keith Richards' piano accompaniment was lost to Connolly's anger crackling electronically across the bar. Max crossed the floor and sat at a table. Thankfully the early doors punters were still in the bookies over the road, but in this mood his boss's unpredictability was a concern. He beckoned furtively and Connolly lurched over and joined him at the table.

"I've had a tip off from the car wash. The accountant has told them he's collecting this afternoon. Me and Non-Stop will be there to meet him." Max lowered his voice and spoke slowly, hoping he could calm his boss down.

"Good boy." Connolly took a swig of whiskey.

"Want us to bring him here?"

"No son. It's Big Ronnie's 50th. Him and the boys from his golf club are coming in later. Take him to the other place, we'll do it on the phone."

Max nodded, but was unsure how that would work, due to Connolly's accent and the fact that he was already two days drunk.

"Sure you don't want to see him face to face boss, might be easier?"

Connolly took a drag on his cigarette and shook his head.

"No time for that. We need to shut this particular problem down quickly. We might have an even bigger one son. Much bigger. The Dutchman rang. The boys never turned up with the bag this morning. After we've dealt with the accountant, I need you to find them and find out what the fuck is going on and where my cash is."

Chapter 14

"I'm sorry love, I haven't heard from him since Tuesday. Wasn't he at the match with you last night? Terrible result that. What happened?"

Christine Yardsley was sitting on her sofa watching Mark 'Danno' Daniels pacing back and forth in front of the fire, scuffling the rug with his feet. She'd slept late after Neil's late night appearance in her bedroom and was still in her dressing gown when Danno had appeared at the door just before midday.

"He went to' toilet at half time then disappeared. When I got back to' flat he was already in bed. Then this morning he'd gone when I got up."

"Well, I wouldn't worry Mark. Maybe he's painting with Dougie?"

"No Mrs Yardsley, he isn't. We had somewhere to go today. Somewhere important. Summat's up, I can tell."

"Sure you don't want a cup of tea love?" Christine could see Danno was in a right fluster. Up and down, back and forth, running his fingers through his fringe. She couldn't help wonder if he was on drugs. Danno shook his head and peered out of the window.

"Are those bloody gypsies still on' moor. Mucky buggers aren't they?"

"Mrs Yardsley..." She was sure there were tears in his eyes as he turned to face her.

"What is it love?"

"I think Stuart's done summat really daft."

"Done what Mark?"

"I think he might have stolen summat from a man we've been working for..."

"He wouldn't do that Mark, he's a good lad. You know that."

"I'm scared Mrs Yardsley. This man..." Danno shook his head and started to sob quietly.

"Oh Mark, don't get upset. I'm sure it's a misunderstanding and he'll understand. What's his name, this man?"

"Connolly. Alan Connolly. He runs a pub in Harehills."

Christine Yardsley stared into the three bars of the fire and despite the heat, felt her hair prickle and the goosebumps form on her arm.

"Is he Scottish, this Connolly? Late forties... likes..."

"....The Rolling Stones? Yes."

Christine Yardsley reached for her mask and gulped air, eyes wide.

"Do you know him then Mrs Yardsley?"

"I used to know him. A long long time ago."

Chapter 15

Friday 27 April 1990

Rushdie is told stop hiding -- Death threat author Salman Rushdie was told today to stop hiding and come out into the open. The challenge came from the leader of the Moslem community of Bradford, where the burning of copies of Rushdie's book 'The Satanic Verses' launched a worldwide protest which resulted in a religious 'fatwa' being declared on the writer.

United's Players Told - Keep Calm -- Howard Wilkinson had a 'keep calm' message for his Second division leaders and a 'stay with us' plea to supporters as he looked forward to tomorrows crucial clash against mid table Leicester City at Elland Road (3pm). The midweek defeat by Barnsley which followed a costly mistake by goalkeeper Mervyn Day was a shock to the system for players and supporters alike and Wilkinson is hoping that neither will be affected by it tomorrow.

Alan Connolly leant on the bar and absent mindedly melted his thumb nail with a lit cigarette. He scowled towards the stage where Big Ronnie and his fat nephew were slurring an accompaniment to Undercover of the Night.

"Fucking heathens," Connolly muttered under his breath as he reached under the bar and withdrew the bayonet from its metal scabbard. He tilted it beneath the bar lights, admiring the glint of the cold steel. Imagining the violence on his father's face as he'd plunged it into the gut of a Japanese conscript in Burma. Twisted it round, making a proper mess of the kid's guts.

"Take no prisoners brother."

Connolly's mind had wandered towards fantasies of running the blade through the back of the fucking fat waste-of-space parading around on his stage, disrespecting the work of his Satanic Majesty, when the phone rang.

"Max?"

"We've got him."

"Who? The boys??"

"No. The accountant. Picked him up at the car wash."

"What about the lads? The Dutchman was on again. They still haven't turned up with the bag."

"Okay, we'll get on that next. Do you want to talk to the accountant?"

"Not really. Just find out what he knows then get rid of him....No Ronnie... for fucks sake, be careful or you'll scratch the bloody record."

"What did you say?" Max was struggling to hear above the boom of the pub's speakers.

"Get him to admit that he's been skimming off the collections, find out where he's put the cash, then get fucking shut of him."

"As in...?"

"Do I have to spell it out Max? Get fucking rid. We've looked at the numbers again and they don't add up. We've had it up to here with cunts ripping us off. It's got to be him. Find out what he knows then get rid...Understand?"

"Erm...yeah. Okay gaffer if you're sure?"

"Course I'm fucking sure. And Max..."

"Boss?"

"Hold the phone near his head. I want to listen."

Alan Connolly lit another cigarette and pulled a stool up to the bar, cradling the receiver between his right ear and shoulder. He felt the chill of the steel on his palm turn warm as blood trickled towards his wrist. He began to nod his head as the first piano notes of Let's Spend the Night Together burst from the speaker. One of the golf club boys had joined Big Ronnie on vocals to belt out the intro... 'Barra-barra, Ba-ba-ba-ra-ra!! Connolly laughed and waved the bayonet like a conductor's baton as he listened to the sounds of a man being tortured to death in a warehouse five miles away.

"Take no fucking prisoners brother." Keith whispered in his ear and Alan Connolly closed his eyes as a contented smile spread across his face.

Chapter 16

"Hiya love, do you know' lads who live in' top flat?" A disembodied female voice over the intercom told Neil she hadn't seen them for a few days.

"Okay thanks, I've put a note through' door with a phone number on. If you see either of them could you ask them to call me urgently?"

Neil had spotted the black XR3i waiting in a visitor's space as soon as he'd arrived to try and locate Stuart and Danno's flat in the red brick development off Grove Lane. The occupants now revealed themselves as two mid-twenties black men. The way they exited the car, scanning the windows of the flats for observers and fanning out on either side of him caused Neil to pause. He momentarily considered making a run for it but after two solid days drinking he thought it unlikely he'd outpace them.

"Who are you then?" The taller of the two, dressed in a Green Adidas tracksuit didn't look like he wanted to make friends.

"Alright lads, just looking for my mate. He lives somewhere in these flats. I'm not sure which block though."

"Name?" The other black lad was conspicuously reaching into the lining of his leather three quarter length jacket.

"Mine or his?" Neil smiled, swaying slightly, his eyes glazed.

"Both." Green tracksuit clearly wasn't in the mood for smalltalk.

"I'm Gary and my mate's Jason. Jason Green. Do you know him?" Neil had always been able to think on his feet when drunk, and the skill now proved very useful.

"Nah."

"Works in' market. Do you live here then? Nice place..."

The two men stood six feet away from Neil and looked him up and down, with the threesome forming a perfect triangle.

"Why did you ring that bell? You know someone in that block?"

"I've only been here once and as you can tell, I've had a good drink lads. I thought it was that one. I think it might be' one over' other side now. They look' same from' road."

Neil walked between the men and they exchanged glances as they stepped back, both seeming to want the other to make a decision on whether Neil was bullshitting them.

"Cheers lads. See you around." Neil rounded the corner onto the main road and set off running.

Chapter 17

Saturday 28th April 1990

Poll Tax Demo in City Centre -- Protestors gathered throughout Leeds today for a mass demonstration against the Poll Tax. As many as 5000 people converged on the city centre for what promised to be the largest march in Leeds for years.

Fake tickets alert-- Police and Leeds United officials were on special alert for today's sell-out home match with Leicester City following the discovery of scores of forged tickets.

"I'm alright Hursty. I'm alright." Neil, unshaven and dishevelled, nursed a can of Stella while sitting at a bench table outside the Waggon.

"You don't look alright pal. How long have you been here?"

"Dunno really. Since the sun came up."

"You're not really kipping in' van?" Hursty looked over his shoulder at Young Sutcliffe and the rest of the lads laughing and making head-tap gestures towards Neil.

"I can't go home mate. My mam lied to me. It's all fucked."

"You been drinking for two days too?"

"Helps me sleep."

"Come on mate, this isn't you. You need to snap out of it. Massive game today, then you can come back and stay at mine for as long as you need."

"It doesn't matter now. Nowt left. No family now..."

"What are you on about?"

"My dad's not my dad, our kid's on a suicide mission and has disappeared, and apparently my mam's going to Australia." Neil began to laugh.

"If you say so pal. I'm going to' offy to get you a bottle of water. You need to sober up or you'll get nicked at' gate."

'Shit or Bust, this year promotion's a must' was the slogan on T-shirts bearing the snarling face of Vinnie Jones, sold by unofficial vendors on Lowfields Road. That had been the feeling all season, and Leeds and Sheffield United had been locked in a season long battle at the top of Division 2. A faltering end to the campaign had left it all to play for with Newcastle breathing down the necks of the two Yorkshire sides. The game against Leicester City was nothing less than a 'must win' and the sun shone as a capacity crowd made their way into the ramshackle old ground. Neil and Hursty were again standing on the South Stand terrace, which was rocking in beer fuelled anticipation long before kick off. Hursty had managed to distract the steward on the turnstile long enough to conceal his friend's drunken state and the packed terrace now at least kept Neil upright, and the frequent crowd surges kept him half awake.

Pre-match nerves were compounded when Leicester won the toss and turned Leeds around, meaning they'd be attacking the Kop end in the first half – an obvious sign of impending doom for the superstitious Leeds fans. The game set off at a predictably breakneck pace with Leeds piling forward and it only took 13 minutes for the deadlock to be broken. A Davison loose ball found its way to the overlapping Sterland on the right wing, who advanced to the edge of the penalty box before unleashing a low, hard drive into the far corner. Elland

Road erupted and it was no surprise to Hursty when he saw Neil disappear under a scrum of bodies tumbling down the terrace.

"Jesus, I could have done without that." Neil rubbed his head after hauling himself upright and re-assuming his position.

"It's a bad day for a hangover." Hursty agreed.

The stadium was living up to it's reputation as a modern day bear-pit with the crowd roaring Leeds on, and only the heroics of Leicester's keeper, Martin Hodge, kept the deficit to a single goal at half time. As the teams emerged for the second half, Neil headed downstairs for some water. Emerging from the toilet, he was nudged from behind and turned to see Danno jogging ahead of him.

"Neil, quick, follow me," Neil headed up the steps behind Danno as he shoved his way through the packed ranks behind the goal.

They stopped in a foot-square half-space, level with the cross bar, and Danno nervously turned to survey the fans around them.

"They're after me," he panted, his eyes flicking and beads of sweat visible in the stubble above his top lip.

"Who? Connolly?"

"His boys, yes. They're here. I can't fucking believe what Stu did. I'm back at my mam's. I daren't go to the flat."

"Have you heard from him?"

"No nowt. You?"

"Not since he told me my dad wasn't my dad and that he was nicking Connolly's cash."

"Cash? I thought it was dope?"

"Cash apparently, and lots of it."

"Oh fucking hell, that's even worse." Danno began to shake visibly as the crowd around them surged forward, and Leicester's winger Oldfield picked up the ball on the left, dodging two Leeds challenges.

"How do you know they're here?"

"They know we come to games so must have been staking the ground out. They saw me near the chip shop then followed me in...oh fuck!"

Oldfield pulled the ball infield and City's highly rated midfielder Mcallister guided a perfect shot into the top corner. It seemed to take the small contingent of Leicester fans a few seconds to register what had happened, before a muted celebration contrasted with the stunned silence of the Leeds fans.

"Well that's fucked it."

Danno continued to swivel on his tiptoes to scan the crowd around him.

"Calm down, you're safe here. How could they spot you in this lot?

"Connolly has contacts all over. How do you think they were able to follow me in? He has coppers working for him and it's all camera'd up in here now. I wouldn't be surprised if he's not sat in' control box in his leather kegs, working' CCTV." Both men laughed, knowing that if they didn't, they'd probably cry.

The game entered its last five minutes with Leeds pushing for the winning goal they so desperately needed. Early leavers, eager to escape the packed car parks or to catch the first P2's to town, started to push past, heading up the terrace to the exits.

"I've never understood how people can leave at this stage of' game" Neil shook his head as Leeds drove forward once more.

The ball was kicked into touch in front of the West Stand and Danno craned his neck as Sterland dashed to collect it. As he watched the bulky full-back shape up to take a long throw, his attention was drawn to a slow moving shape in the near distance. A huge man, forging a path through the densely packed crowd ahead.

Sterland released the ball as Danno made eye contact with the approaching giant. Non-Stop Nigel.

"Oh shit!" Danno turned, as a Leicester defender miss-hit the ball and it bounced out to Strachan.

The crowd surged forward and the ball bobbled around near the penalty spot, as Danno spotted Max and one of Connolly's Chapeltown lads piling down the terrace towards him.

The ball hit Strachan, then bounced to Speed who knocked it back into the path of the Leeds captain.

"Come here you little fucker!" Max lunged towards Danno as the ball fizzed off Strachan's foot. Danno never saw the goal, but for him, there had never been one better timed. The entire South Stand seemed to rise as one, like a bouncing, multi-headed entity of ten thousand raised arms. Strachan's momentum carried him towards the fence and for a moment it seemed that he'd carry on into the celebrating masses behind the goal, or that they'd join him on the pitch. Fans were scaling the fences and the police struggled to maintain control as jubilant supporters danced, hugged and sang.

A veteran of terrace celebrations, Danno knew exactly how to ride the wave of euphoria and emerged twenty feet from where he'd begun. He looked back across the terrace to see Non-Stop Nigel throwing punches at fans who'd made a big mistake in involving him in their celebrations, as Neil shrank away into the crowd.

The final whistle sounded and fans flooded onto the pitch, providing the additional cover needed for Danno to make his escape.

In the centre circle, Neil spotted Hursty and the lads, and joined them in waiting for the other results. After some Vinnie Jones inspired confusion which led them to believe they'd been promoted, the actual results were announced over the tannoy. Newcastle and Sheffield had both won. The race for promotion would go to the final game.

"Bournemouth it is then. I reckon half of Leeds is going to be down there next weekend." Hursty slapped Neil on the back and grinned in anticipation of a bank holiday weekend on the south coast.

Chapter 18

"Don't you worry Julie, I can cope for a couple of days, I've got stuff in' freezer." Christine Yardsley sat with the phone on her knee, the extension cord at maximum length from its position on the window sill.

*

"And they didn't take owt then apart from some cash? Just trashed the place? I bet it were druggies. Little buggers. They need birching then locking up."

*

"No love, I've not seen either of them. Not spoken to Neil since Wednesday night's upset, I've no idea where he is. And nowt from Stuart since his pal came round on Thursday and frightened me to death."

*

"I have. I've left three messages at the flat but he hasn't rung back. I feel so helpless just sat here when Stuart's in trouble and Neil obviously hates me."

*

"I will love. Look, don't you bother about me. Let me know what' police say when they come, and I hope you get it all tidied up."

*

"And you Julie. Bye love, bye."

Christine Yardsley slowly pulled herself from the sofa and shuffled over to the window. Everyone's gone now. Even the bloody gypsies.

Chapter 19

Julie Statham put down the phone and slumped cross legged on the floor of her small semi in a neat cul-de-sac in Garforth, amidst the debris of her kitchen cupboards. Every packet, box and jar had been opened, with the contents strewn across the furniture and smeared on the walls. A grocery explosion of tea and coffee, cooking sauces, breakfast cereals, pot noodles. Ruined house, ruined marriage, ruined life.

She hauled herself from the floor, muscles stiff after two hours on the lino, staring at the mess through her tears. Into the living room, a blizzard of sofa foam and paper. The concertina file she'd taken from the office, upturned and contents torn and scattered. Reminders and mortgage arrears letters, their red ink bright amongst the bank statements, her nursing qualification certificate and all the birthday and Valentine cards she and Richard had ever sent each other.

Up a staircase of paper, into the bedroom. Their bed, mattress with springs bared, like a rotting carcass. Clothes slashed and discarded, her best underwear carefully placed centre stage made her shiver.

'Let me know what the police say'. What would they say, if she called them? If she let them in, two disinterested local bobbies who'd tap the patio doors and shake their heads and tell her how easy they are to get through. Who'd ask what was taken, then why there was £750 in cash in the house in the first place. What her husband actually did for a living, and why she hadn't seen him since he left for work on Thursday. Whether she thought it was normal that he often disappeared for days at a time, then flew into a rage when she asked him about it. What she thought the burglars were looking for, and why they'd targeted her house.

No, the police wouldn't say anything because she wouldn't tell them. This was for her and Richard to sort out once and for all. This time when he came back, they'd sit down and talk properly. She'd make him admit he was gambling again, and they'd get him some help. She'd ask about his job and he'd tell her everything. No more secrets.

Julie headed back downstairs feeling more positive.

"Marmaduke....Marmaduke...psssss psssss psssss." She'd trained him to use a litter tray and he only left the house to bask in the sun on the patio on a rare cloudless day. Poor boy must have been terrified when a stranger appeared and started trashing his home.

Julie dodged the rotary drier and crossed the small back lawn to the shed. She couldn't remember the last time she'd been in there, and tugged open the door expecting to see two unused mountain bikes and a flymo, bought as a house-warming gift by Richard's parents.

It was the small pink tongue she spotted first, extending for more than an inch, beneath a little black nose positioned at her eye level, less than a metre in front of her as she opened the door. Suspended by a length of electrical cable which had been pulled taut around his neck, Marmaduke revolved slowly, his limbs stiffened at right angles by the contortions of his slow death throes.

It was only as Julie hacked at the electrical flex with garden shears to send Marmaduke thudding onto the shed floor, that it occurred to her that she may never see her husband again.

Chapter 20

Monday 30th April 1990

Fear of 'Mind-Bend' Drugs Craze Grows - Drugs seizures have reinforced police fears of a dramatic rise in the use of LSD - The 'fashionable' drug of the sixties. And one leading expert says that mind-bending LSD is prevalent in Leeds, particularly among young people frequenting the city's night clubs.

"Must be his wife. She's a pretty lassie right enough. If yus two had any fucking brains you'd have searched his wallet before you topped him. Reckon he'd have talked if we'd brought her here for a wee duet with Uncle Alan." Alan Connolly surveyed the contents of the accountant's wallet spread on the bar before him.

"I take it she wasn't around when yus went to the house?"

"We waited till she went out gaffer. We wanted to avoid any drama."

"And you tipped the place upside down and only found this?" Connolly fingered a bundle of cash, wrapped in a rubber band.

"Looked everywhere boss. Ripped the mattresses open, took the bath apart, even checked the shed. Only that bundle of cash and no paperwork."

"Wee bastard..." Connolly muttered and took a swig of Jamesons.

"And Evrol, Steve...no luck finding the boys?"

"No boss, we waited at the flat all afternoon. A few comings and goings but not them. It's a security door too so we can't get in to search the flat without being seen. We think we might know where the Daniels kid works through."

"Good. All of you get on that. We've chopped off one snake's head but I need my cash back before we do the same to the other two."

Chapter 21

"Hello Mrs Daniels, it's Stuart. Is Mark there?"

*

"Flood at the flat...? What...ah, yeah...Yes I'm back at my mum's too. Nightmare eh? I bet he is. Sorry but I'm on a pay phone so I'll need to be quick."

*

"Thanks."

*

"Danno, it's me....."

*

"I know, I know and I'm sorry. I really am."

*

"They don't know where we live though..."

*

"Yeah I suppose they could, but I doubt it. Better safe than sorry I suppose. I'm really sorry mate, honestly I am."

*

"I can't tell you. It's safer if you don't know. I'm alright though, well out of the way."

*

"Danno...just shut up a minute. I'm on a payphone so I need to be quick. Look, I did it for a reason and I'll explain when I see you. It was for my mum, but it will set me and you up too. Just wait till the weekend."

*

"Yeah. Bournemouth. Course I am. That's what I'm ringing about. Did you get them?

*

"Fucking sound mate! You didn't think I'd miss this one did you? It's going to be fucking mad down there. And I'll explain everything then. When we've won' game we can have a proper promotion party down there."

*

"Sorry Danno...the pips are going. I'm gonna have to go. Leeds end turnstile at two, right? See you there pal. Stay safe!"

*

Chapter 22

Wednesday 2 May 1990

16 Held in Police Swoops -- 16 people were arrested in a series of early morning raids on homes in South Leeds today. Sixty officers took part in Operation Airburst which centred mainly on addresses in the Beeston area. Police later revealed that in addition to 16 men being arrested, they also seized property valued at £5000 including motorcycles, golf clubs, CD and video players and car radios.

Venues Lined up for Live Screening -- Leeds United's fight to the finish promotion clash at Bournemouth on Saturday is to be screened live to four venues in the city, it was revealed today. Demand for the 2000 match tickets available to United supporters for the end of season thriller massively outweighs supply, and today it was announced that the game will be beamed back live to fans at The Astoria ballroom, Roundhay Road; The Refectory at Leeds University; Armley Sports centre and The Civic Theatre in Leeds.

"Mrs Daniels? I'm Neil, Stuart's brother. How's Mark?" Neil hated hospitals at the best of times, but the overheated, painted brick, disinfectant stinking, Victorian corridors of Leeds General Infirmary were giving him prison flashbacks.

"You took some tracking down. I must have rung half the lads in South Leeds when your mam said she didn't know where you or Stuart were." The smartly dressed, late forties woman turned from her bedside seat and gave him a disapproving look.

"I'm sorry. I've been moving about a bit. How is he?"

"Sedated for the pain. Not making much sense but he knows where he is."

"Do they know what happened?"

"I was hoping you might be able to tell me? He never turned up for work yesterday, his boss rang to ask where he was. I said he'd set off as usual. Next thing I knew I got a call from the police saying he'd been found attacked in his flat. They think he may have gone back and disturbed burglars and they've given him a right good hiding."

"Jesus." Neil tried to avert his gaze from Danno's lower legs which were wrapped in thick white gauze bandages, now mottled with seaping crimson.

"Funny thing though. He'd moved back to my house because they'd had a flood at the flat, but the police say there was no sign of one. Also your mam said Stuart hasn't moved back there. I don't understand that...and when he came round, the first thing he said was to contact you. What the hell's going on?"

"I'm really sorry Mrs Daniels, I don't know either." Danno's mother looked at Neil suspiciously then stood and picked up her handbag.

"I've been here all morning. I'm going for a cuppa. You want anything?"

"No I'm fine thanks." Neil took her place beside Danno's bed and recoiled at the smell of dry blood and antiseptic. He watched as she hurried from the ward, stopping to speak to a nurse as she left. They both turned and gave him a critical stare.

"Danno...Danno. It's Neil. Are you awake?" Danno's eyes flickered and he licked his lips and gasped.

"Water." Neil poured a plastic glass from a jug on the bedside cabinet and held it to Danno's parched lips.

"Help me up." Danno croaked and grimaced as Neil hoisted him higher up the stack of pillows.

"What the fuck mate..?"

Danno took a deep breath and screwed up his face in pain as he tried to move his legs.

"I've done a bad thing Neil, really bad..." A loud inhalation morphed into a sob and tears filled Danno's eyes.

"Go on mate, whatever it is, we can sort it..."

Danno was shaking his head and covering his face with shaking hands.

"They got me. Connolly and those fucking gorillas who work for him. I parked my car round' corner from work, next thing I know I'm in' back of a van with a bag on my head." Tears were pouring down Danno's cheeks now and his loud sobs attracted the attention of patients at the other side of the ward.

"I thought I was going to die Neil. I knew it was them but none of them spoke. That made it worse. I pissed and shit myself, and that really wound Connolly up. He started poking me in the throat with that bayonet he carries." Danno raised his chin and pointed to a centimetre long cut next to his Adam's apple.

"They took me to an empty warehouse, I don't know where, and sat me on a chair...." Danno was now shaking uncontrollably.

"It's okay mate, you're safe now."

"They pulled' bag off my head and I was sat surrounded by a fucking big pool of blood. It was like they'd killed a fucking cow or summat in there. And he, Connolly, says this is what happens to cunts who rip us off. Then Non-Stop Nigel pulled' chair away and I was sliding around in' blood on' floor. It fucking stank Neil, oh Jesus, I can still smell it..." Danno covered his eyes and rocked in his hospital bed. Neil Yardsley felt nausea rising in his chest as he realised just what his brother had got into.

"I was covered in blood, it was freezing cold and sticky so it wasn't fresh. It smelt so bad I puked up. So I'd pissed and shit myself and was covered in vomit too. Connolly lost it. Started asking me where his bag was. I said I knew nowt about it and didn't know where Stu was. He told Non-Stop to hold me down and they took my trainers off. He started going on about how he'd stop me dancing when I was meant to be working. He took my socks off and I could see Max and the others looking at each other, like, what the fuck is he doing, and I could see him waving the bayonet about. By now I was struggling and Non-Stop was holding me down and he was covered in blood too..."

Neil realised he'd involuntarily raised his hand to cover his mouth as the full horror of Danno's ordeal became apparent. He cast a nervous eye towards the ward door in case his mother returned.

"Go on mate..."

"Connolly was shouting 'hold him still' and I felt this pain in my big toe....He started trying to cut my toe off with the bayonet. I don't know what happened, I think I blacked out then. It all went weird. Next thing I knew I could hear screaming, really loud screaming, then I realised it was me. I couldn't feel my feet. I opened my eyes and Connolly was stood there, covered in blood with a hammer in his hand. He said 'try dancing now you little cunt.'"

"Fucking hell, Danno. I don't know what to say."

"That's not the end of it though. I was passing out, in a right state. They shoved summat up my nose, poppers or summat and I came round a bit. I was just in my boxers on the floor. Next thing I knew, Max is stood there with a big hose pipe. He shouted turn it on, and this huge jet of water blew me into the corner and I just lay there with it battering me against the wall. They think it's broke about three ribs, but at least it washed all the blood and shit off me. I remember laying there shivering, thinking I was going to die. Next thing I knew, I woke up back in' flat, I don't remember them taking me there. The place was trashed and the pain in my feet was unbelievable, and Connolly was stood there with his bayonet, grinning. He said 'If you don't want to die here, you'll tell us where the money is hidden.' I knew he meant it Neil, they were going to kill me. I'm sorry...I'm so sorry."

"You told him where Stu is?"

"No I couldn't. I don't know. But yes, I was so scared I would have done. I'm sorry...so, so sorry."

"It's okay mate. What did you tell them?"

"Where I've arranged to meet him."

"Go on pal..."

"Bournemouth. Outside' Leeds end on Saturday at two. Tickets are in my wallet if you want them. I'm not likely to be going anywhere soon. You have to go warn him Neil. They're going to kill him. Please, you have to find him before they do. If not, he's dead."

Chapter 23

Thursday 3rd May 1990

Yorkshire Cricket in TV Race Rumpus --Yorkshire County Cricket Club was at the centre of a race row today following comments made on TV by senior member Brian Close. The club was featured in a BBC documentary 'The Race Game' which examined attitudes to race within all aspects of sport. Mr Close, chairman of the club's cricket committee was asked in an interview why no Yorkshire born black or Asian players had ever been picked to play for the county. He replied that none had ever been good enough to play 1st class cricket.

£100 Bid to See Big Match -- Leeds United fans travelling to Bournemouth for Saturday's promotion deciding match are said to be paying more than £100 a time for Bournemouth AFC tickets and members cards in a bid to gain entry to Dean Court. Leeds United administration manager Alan Roberts said he had seen tickets to areas of the ground reserved for Bournemouth supporters purchased by United fans at vastly inflated prices.

"Is that you Julie?" the sound of the latch clicking roused Christine Yardsley from her snooze.

"Julie...love...?"

Christine hadn't seen Julie all week but didn't want to call her office in case they didn't realise she was off. Poor lass had enough problems without getting into trouble at work. Supplies in the freezer were getting low and Christine had been having her tea with no milk for two days, but that was forgotten when her eldest son's head appeared round the corner of the door.

"Neil! Where've you been love?"

"Hi mam. I've been staying at a Hursty's. Thought it best I get away for a few days..."

"Oh Neil, I'm so sorry love. I made a terrible mistake. I should have told you..."

"It's alright mam. It was a shock that's all. I've had time to think now. We can sit down and talk about it properly another time, but I'm in a rush now. Hursty is waiting for me in' van. I just need to pick up a few things."

Neil squeezed his mother's hand then disappeared into the back bedroom where she could hear him pulling his old Head bag out of the wardrobe.

"I don't know what I was thinking..." Christine called, her voice too soft to hear. When Neil returned she was crying.

"Look mam, my dad was Dennis Yardsley and that hasn't changed. On the day he died he made me promise to look after you and Stu, and that's what I'm going to do." He knelt in front of his mother and took hold of her hands.

"Stu's in trouble mum, big trouble. He's going to walk into a trap in Bournemouth at' weekend and I need to get to him first to warn him. If he calls here, tell him to keep his head down and stay away from' ground on Saturday. We're kipping in the van so I've no way for him to contact me. Tell him I'll wait at' end of ' pier at seven tomorrow night."

"What if he doesn't call?

"I'll have to try and catch him at' ground. Let's hope it doesn't come to that though."

"You're scaring me Neil. What's he done? Is it that man he works for who's after him? What are you going to do?"

"He's done summat stupid and he needs to make it right. I'll help him but I need to find him before they do. I'll do whatever it takes mam. I made a promise to dad." Neil stood up and picked up his bag.

"No Neil, please don't go down there, not with that man, please Neil, please..."

He was already out of the door and heading to the ground floor three steps at a time. Downstairs he dodged the dogshit on the scrubby grass verge in front of the flats, and jumped the small wall. Hursty had the window open.

"Alright? Where to...?

"Birch Services. Summat to collect for Bournemouth."

Chapter 24

"Bournemouth here we come! Get your bags packed boys, we're off to the seaside." Alan Connolly replaced the receiver and addressed four blank faces at the table in front of the bar.

"I've got us on a mini-bus tomorrow morning with the old LS9 Asylum lads. You're gonna hear some proper tales of going to the football in the 70's. Fuck me, we had some real tear-ups..." Connolly slid his father's bayonet from its scabbard and grinned as he sliced the throat of a long forgotten Man United fan.

"Tomorrow gaffer? I thought the match was Saturday? Why don't we just get down there at two and pick the kid up at the ground?"

"What's the matter with you Max, have you got a date tomorrow?" Evrol and Steve smirked and Non-Stop Nigel stared impassively at his boss.

"No but it's a long way on a bus. And where are we sleeping?"

"The bus will be a fucking riot son, I've got my Stones mix cassettes out already. And as a responsible employer I've secured us two rooms at the High Cliff Hotel. One's a double for me and you, and you three are in the single." All four men at the table looked at each other with puzzled expressions.

"Maybe bring some vaseline eh Maxy?" Connolly winked at his young henchman.

Chapter 25

Friday 4 May 1990

'The Heat is on' say May Day Met Men--Weather experts were today blowing hot and cold over predictions for Bank Holiday sunshine. Met men in Leeds are predicting an end to the heatwave over the weekend and cooler temperatures, but their colleagues in London forecast a sizzling May Day Bank Holiday for the South.

United Head to South Coast Hideaway -- Howard Wilkinson took his first team squad to a South Coast hideaway to 'get away from it all' before the crucial promotion encounter with relegation threatened Bournemouth at Dean Court on Saturday. United have no injury worries for a game which both teams need to win to achieve their very different aims, without relying on other results going in their favour.

The morning dawned bright and across the city of Leeds, an army was on the move. In uniform of shorts and t-shirts, with holdalls slung over shoulders, the forces of Leeds United were mobilising. In the car parks of early-opening supermarkets, crates of beer were loaded into car boots; in cafes across the city, the usual Friday coffee morning pensioners shook their heads at noisy tables of lads tucking into a full English; coaches and mini-buses were jet washed in preparation for the long journey south; pubs designated as pick-up points buzzed like a Saturday night as the first pints of the Bank Holiday weekend were downed and battle anthems rehearsed. *When we win promotion, this is what we'll sing...*

Neil snoozed in the back of Hursty's works van, his head resting on his bag. They were travelling in convoy –

twenty of them in two transits, the lads in the back of each van slumped on sleeping bags with Head-bag pillows. Neil squeezed his hold-all until he located the bulge of the package he'd collected from one of his Liverpool contacts at the M62 services. A pistol wrapped in a towel. A starting pistol converted to fire live rounds but Scouse John had assured him that 'if you get close enough it will do the job la'. Neil had sworn Hursty to secrecy so none of the lads in the van knew what he was carrying. If all went to plan, no one ever need know of the gun's existence. If it didn't go to plan, nothing mattered anyway.

The van horn was sounded with increasing regularity as other vans, cars and buses were identified as Leeds fans heading south on the M1 and were greeted with Leeds salutes from the outside lane. It felt like the whole of the city was making its way to Bournemouth, and many of those travelling hadn't seen the team play live since relegation eight years earlier. Others hadn't been to a game since the Revie era. Two Thursday night Britannia drinkers had secured places in Hursty's van after hearing about the trip the previous evening. They'd be joining thousands of others in calling in sick to join the party.

It was lunchtime when the convoy reached Bournemouth and pulled into a car park across the road from the beach. It was clear from the number of Salford Van Hire and Albert Rentals vans already parked up that the 'No overnight camping' signs would be obsolete this weekend. Within minutes of arriving, Young Sutcliffe was leading the occupants of his van towards the beer-soaked strains of Marching on Together, being carried on the breeze from a big pub with a beer garden near the pier.

The temperature was already nudging the high 70's and the search for ale and tickets was the obvious priority for most of the lads now.

"I'll catch you later Hursty. I'm going for a mooch to see if I can spot our kid. Keep your eye out won't you?"

Hursty replied with a thumbs up before jogging after the rest of the van. It was just after 1pm and Leeds invasion of Bournemouth had begun.

Chapter 26

Chief Inspector Roger Thorpe blinked through exhaled smoke as he watched four men clamber, stretching, out of a black Ford Granada in the car park of Dorset police headquarters. Grinning beneath their moustaches, joking, clutching their weekend bags. All smiles, looking forward to their jolly boys bank holiday weekend at the coast. A weekend that he should have spent sailing with Carol and their friends Keith and Susan, before he was nominated Gold Commander for a football match. A football match which shouldn't even be happening. A game which the politicians and senior officers had asked to be moved as soon as it was scheduled by the football league's mythical fixtures computer. Leeds United, the team with the biggest following in the 2nd tier, not to mention a highly organised hooligan element, playing their final game of the season at a tiny stadium, better suited to 4th division football, and on a Spring Bank Holiday weekend. That was bad enough, but now the game was one they had to win. A game which could clinch them the championship and send them back to the top division for the first time in eight years. Even when that had become a likely scenario, the powers-that-be had still declined to move the game.

"Just deal with it. It's only football fans, not the IRA," the Chief Super had told him, and his weekend's leave was cancelled, just like that. Fuck you. Career copper. Politician's lapdog.

"The West Yorkshire liaison team have arrived sir." Janet's tight curly perm appeared around the door corner.

"Send Morgan down to meet them, please, I'm busy."

Roger Thorpe, thirty five years in the job, eight months from retirement, lit another cigarette and flicked open the cover of Sailing Today. Perfect weather and the chance of a first weekend off in two months. Instead he'd be dealing with hordes of drunken, northern scum sleeping on his town's beaches and pissing in its shop doorways. Drug addicted ravers gulping down LSD tablets. The infamous Service Crew in their expensive sweaters and deerstalker hats with Stanley knives concealed in their socks. Yorkshire miners who still bore a grudge. The football league's fictitious computer had despatched the worst thugs in football to his seaside town on a bank holiday, just as it had to Cleethorpes in 82, Yarmouth in 86 and Brighton in 87, and he was the one who would have to handle the inevitable fallout. The perfect storm.

Roger Thorpe watched Morgan shaking hands with the Yorkshire liaison team in the car park below and put out his cigarette on the window.

"Fuck you. Fuck you all."

Chapter 27

"My god, what has he got on?" Max, Evrol, Steve and Non-Stop Nigel were sat at a bench table outside a pub on the edge of Bournemouth city centre. A loud cheer erupted from the rest of the LS9 Asylum lads as they spotted Alan Connolly bowling down the road towards them.

Max shook his head. A five hour bus journey listening to his boss recount tales of sawn-off shotguns in Stanley Park; wading into the scum with a hammer at Hillsborough 77; and blinding the Paris CRS with their own tear gas in 75 wasn't his idea of a fun Friday. And now Connolly had come out for the night dressed like Kid Creole. A cream suit with baggy, peg-top trousers, low cut turquoise t-shirt and matching espadrilles, obviously sockless, it was clear what someone was going to comment as he crossed the road, and Market Dave was the unfortunate culprit.

"Wahey, it's Don Johnson!"

"What's that you say son?"

"Don Johnson. Miami Vice." Dave was still laughing when he saw the bayonet sliding from the lining of the jacket.

"Who's John Johnson?" Connolly carefully placed the weapon on top of Market Dave's ear, and a couple of senior Asylum members leapt to their feet in an attempt to prevent the first blood of the weekend being spilt before their first pints had been drunk.

"Woah! Alan, Alan...Don Johnson. He's an actor.'" Legendary 70's hooligan Frank Meadows was playing peace maker.

"Is he a poofter or a weirdo?"

"No, is he fuck Alan. He's a proper cool dude. Birds love him. You look...great."

"Aye, you look good Alan, I didn't mean owt bad. It were a complement, honestly." Market Dave slowly raised his hand and eased the bayonet away from his face.

"We're on holiday aren't we boys? Got to look the part." Connolly straightened his jacket and winked at Max.

"Right, let's go for a few pints, then I've lined up a treat for us later. Chinese restaurant with a juke box that shows you the words as you sing along. First one outside London!" Connolly carefully slid the bayonet back into his jacket and pointed the way towards the town centre.

"I've a feeling it's going to be a lively night boys!"

Chapter 28

"Christine, it's me. I've brought the shopping you wanted." Julie Statham immediately noticed the silence in the flat as she turned the key in the lock and pushed open the door. Christine lived her life to a soundtrack of daytime ITV or Radio Aire. But today there was neither. Julie dropped the Safeway bags in the kitchen and peered round the door frame towards the empty sofa.

"Christine? Are you okay? Where are you?"

The faint sound of a bed creaking led her to a door on the right, which she gently opened and peered into the gloom.

"In here Julie love."

"Oh Christine, are you ill?"

"No." Christine Yardsley pulled the quilt over her head and sunk down into the pillows.

"What's up then? It's three o'clock, what are you still in bed for you daft thing?" Julie pulled open the curtains and sunlight streamed into the room.

"I can't face it Julie, I just can't..." Christine began crying and Julie perched on the side of the bed and gently tugged back the duvet.

"What's happened? I'm so sorry I haven't been. I had to take a few days off, what with the break in and Richard..."

"Don't worry love you're here now, and brought my stuff?"

"Yes I got what you asked for. Now what's up? Tell me what's happened."

Christine Yardsley pulled herself upright and reached for the mask on the bedside table.

"Turn the bottle on please love." Julie twisted the dial on the metal cylinder and Christine inhaled deeply then removed her mask and spoke in a hushed voice.

"Stuart's in trouble. He's going to Bournemouth for' match but someone's after him, a really bad person. Neil has gone to try to warn Stuart and stop this bloke. I'm scared Julie. Really scared. The look in Neil's eyes. I'm not sure what he'll do."

"What are they after Stuart for?"

"I don't know exactly. He worked for this man and now he thinks Stuart has stolen summat from him."

"I wouldn't worry, I'm sure when Neil gets there he'll help Stuart sort it out with this fella. They might all end up watching the game together and having a laugh about it..." Christine's expression told Julie she was seriously underestimating the situation.

"I know this man. Or I did, years ago. He's really bad news. Oh Julie..." Christine dissolved into sobs and pulled the duvet over her face.

"What is it? Come on Christine, you can tell me..."

A deep sigh preceded the lowering of the quilt and Christine Yardsley's tear stained, crumpled face appeared.

"The man...Alan Connolly..."

"I don't know him." Julie shook her head, unaware of what was coming.

"Alan Connolly was...is...someone...." Christine shook her head and took a deep breath.

"Connolly is Neil's dad! Neil's real dad. Oh god, Julie, what if Neil goes to Bournemouth and attacks his own father without knowing who he is? What if he kills him? What if Connolly kills Neil or Stu...or both of them?" Christine Yardsley pulled the duvet over her face and howled. A terrible, heart rending cry from deep within her chest that made Julie shiver.

"I'll go make us a cup of tea, you get yourself up. It will make you feel better." Julie squeezed Christine's hand and headed to the kitchen.

Twenty minutes later, now dressed and hair pulled into a semblance of normality, and with a cup of tea clasped in a shaky hand, Christine Yardsley recounted her story.

"It was the mid 60's, I was a teenager. It was different then, we didn't have discos or these raves they go to now. We used to meet in coffee bars in town. The Tropica off Boar Lane and the Del Rio behind Schofields were my favourites. For dancing we used to go to the BG Club and' Three Coins on Albion Walk where' Bond Street centre is now. It was all very innocent. If I got a lift home on a Lambretta I'd get' lad to drop me off at' end of' road as my mum was really strict, and forbid me from riding on motorbikes, as she called them. Anyway, there were these two Scottish brothers, Alan and Keith, and I started seeing Alan. They used to sell pills in' clubs. Not drugs really, just stuff to help kids dance all night. They always had really smart suits and Keith had this scooter with loads of mirrors and lamps. He used to let Alan borrow it to take me home. Alan loved' Rolling Stones. I can still picture him doing his Mick Jagger dance. He even got me a ticket when they played at' Queen's Hall in

1964. I wasn't bothered for' Stones but I liked Lulu. She was' support act." A distant memory caused a semi-smile to flicker momentarily across Christine's pursed lips.

"Anyway, one night Alan got into a fight at a party and stabbed a lad and got locked up. A week later I found out I was pregnant. I was 18. I had Neil in 1965 and Alan kept in touch while he was in jail, but by' time he got out in 67, I'd already met Dennis. Alan saw Neil a couple of times and gave me a few quid to buy him some clothes and stuff, but Dennis thought it best we cut ties altogether. The last time I saw Alan was about 1970, then I heard he went back to jail. Next time I heard his name was this week, when I found out he was going to kill my youngest son." The tears began to flow again as Julie struggled to come up with anything to make the situation sound any better.

"So Alan doesn't know who Stuart and Neil are? Doesn't know you're their mum?"

"How could he? I was called Harrison when he knew me. We didn't mix in the same circles when he came out of jail. He was a young lad. Probably glad to be shut of a girl with a little kid in tow. What a bloody mess!"

As far as Julie could see, there was only one possible solution.

"Don't worry Christine. I'll go there." She stood up.

"Go where?"

"I'll drive down to Bournemouth. Go find Neil and tell him the truth about his dad. Maybe then me and him can find Stuart and go see this Connolly guy and try and work things out. "

"You can't love. I don't know where Neil is. He's kipping in a van somewhere. He didn't tell me owt. All I know is he said to tell Stu to meet him at the pier at seven if he called, but he hasn't."

Julie looked at her watch. Half three. No chance of getting down there for seven, but if Stuart hadn't picked up the message and didn't turn up tonight, surely Neil would head to the pier tomorrow night too. Or perhaps she could find one or both of the brothers in Bournemouth. As far as she knew it wasn't a big town.

"I want to help Christine. I can't think what else to do." The truth was, the house didn't feel the same since the burglary and Richard's vanishing act. The mound of earth by the back fence brought back images of Marmaduke swinging in the shed doorway, and caused her to gulp back tears every time she looked out of the kitchen window.

"But it's so far love. You'll be away all weekend. What about your husband?"

Julie shook her head. "That's another story, you don't need to worry about that. I'll go home and pack a bag and set off. I'll be down there for midnight."

"Thanks so much Julie, you're a true friend," Christine called as she turned to leave.

"And Julie, be careful love, I've got this awful feeling summat really bad is going to happen down in Bournemouth this weekend."

Chapter 29

When Bournemouth's Art Deco Pavilion Theatre was built it occupied an enviable position facing the towns pier, adjacent to the landscaped lower gardens. Recent years had seen the view from the terrace obscured by a flyover carrying the main road from the BIC towards Boscombe, and the theatre bar's latest incarnation was the Holiday Revival pub. With it's large, flagged beer garden bathed in the early evening sunshine it was an obvious focal point for the gathering Leeds hordes.

Chief Inspector Roger Thorpe stepped from his unmarked Cavalier and looked towards the English Channel, glistening beyond the pier. A light breeze blowing around seven knots from the East and a twelve second swell. Perfect sailing conditions. Except he wasn't out there, he was stuck here, with the bare-chested northern hooligans and nervous local police. He peeled his white shirt from his sweat-soaked back and retrieved his jacket from the backseat, then his cap with the oak leaf braiding from the front. He could already hear the moronic chanting from the pub terrace as he headed towards a group of early middle-aged men standing beside a cluster of parked police vehicles.

'Wherever we go, we fear no foe.' Roger Thorpe felt a rivulet of sweat trickle down his back as the officers turned to greet him.

'For we are the YRA. Y-R-A.'

"Afternoon sir, these are the West Yorkshire Intelligence officers. This is Andy Barton, he's in charge." Sergeant Morgan led the introductions.

A man in his late 30's with a moustache and wearing a pink polo shirt extended his hand. Roger Thorpe touched it lightly, reducing any risk of Barton's thumb pressing on his knuckle to reveal himself as a fellow travelling man. He didn't look the type of brother who'd be welcomed in any Dorset lodge.

'We're Yorkshire's Republican Army, we're barmy.'

Standing on the tables, bare chested, arms aloft, goading, challenging.

"Afternoon Sergeant. What's the situation?"

"There are a number of risk targets currently in this public house sir, and we're tracking others on the motorway."

Thorpe's lip curled slightly as he surveyed Barton's outfit. Logoed shirt, faded jeans and white Nike training shoes. Fucking intelligence.

"Show me them please."

Barton paused and looked at Morgan for guidance.

"I can show you our files sir, they're in the car."

"Files? I don't want to see files Sergeant, I want to see the thugs themselves, the leaders of the Service Group. I want to look the cowards in their eyes."

"Erm, we think it's better to maintain surveillance from a distance at present sir. Contain them here..." Morgan had clearly been influenced by his new friends from the north.

"Oh, that's what you think is it, Morgan?"

Morgan fell silent and the group shuffled their feet awkwardly as Roger Thorpe stared towards the packed terrace of the Holiday Revival pub.

"I shouldn't even be here," Thorpe muttered, too quiet for them to hear, then set off towards the pub.

"Chief Inspector, with respect sir, we've put years of work into the football liaison unit at West Yorkshire and our experience tells us..." Roger Thorpe turned to face Barton who was scurrying in his wake.

"Are you scared Sergeant?"

"I'm sorry sir?"

"Are you scared to enter a public house because of the presence of known offenders?"

"No sir, but..."

"It seems to me that the current political preference is to indulge these thugs and afford them a respect they quite frankly don't deserve, via highly paid officers such as yourself 'infiltrating' their ranks. Observing them, analysing them and trying to understand them, rather than getting in there and ruddy well sorting them out!"

"It's not as simple as that sir. Believe me, I've spent the last five years..." Roger Thorpe waived an arm to silence Barton, and walked to the perimeter of the beer garden which was surrounded by a wire fence. He was in no need of intelligence recorded in files by police officers mingling in pubs with low grade criminals. No need for the rules and recommendations imposed a few years earlier by PACE which had effectively tied his hands behind his back. Thirty five years in the force provided all the insight he needed as he surveyed the massed ranks of Leeds supporters and took stock of the situation. Assessed the enemy, using old fashioned copper's intuition, not fucking files locked in a car boot.

The followers. Young, excitable, standing on tables, pints in hands, arms extended, chanting. Stripped to the waist with skinny ribs and sun scorched backs. Three quarter length shorts and sun hats in yellow, blue and white.

The drinkers. Older, fatter, balder. Standing on the benches, daren't risk a table. Leeds shirts, beer bellies and tattoos. Joining in the chants but can't remember the words.

The leaders. The generals. Mid-twenties to thirties. Polo shirts and logoed t-shirts, smart shorts and new white trainers. Standing on the periphery. Not singing. Watching, waiting.

"Always speak to the organ grinders, not the monkeys." Roger Thorpe waved his officers to follow as he headed through the gate to the terrace.

"Sir, I really don't think this is a good idea."

'Who the fuck, who the fuck, who the fucking hell are you?'

Roger Thorpe, thirty five years in the force, eight months from retirement, should be sailing this weekend, ducked as a pint glass missed the top of his cap by inches. The fact that the pub was using real glasses only became apparent as the second missile looped through the cloudless blue sky and shattered at his feet.

"Morgan, why are they not using plastic glasses?" Thorpe turned to see his men back-pedalling as the flurry of missiles became a sustained barrage.

'We're the best behaved supporters in the land... when we win!'

"Officers, stand your ground!" The splash of warm lager on his perspiring face brought an unexpected split second of relief from the heat, but a half-full bottle bouncing off his shoulder made Thorpe's decision to retreat easier.

'We're a right set of bastards when we lose...win or draw!'

Back at the vehicles, Barton was scowling at beer stains down the front of his polo shirt. Thorpe turned away to avoid the obvious 'told you so' glare.

"Pass me a radio Morgan." Roger Thorpe removed his beer soaked jacket and placed it on the car bonnet. Gazing towards the blue ocean he spotted a Windmill dinghy making five knots towards the horizon. Shouldn't even be here.

"Control, this is Chief Inspector Thorpe. We have a code zero at the Holiday Revival pub. I need all available officers deployed immediately in full riot equipment. Get me some canine units down here too."

Morgan and the West Yorkshire officers looked at each other and grimaced. The plan to keep the main body of fans contained on the sea front had seemed to be working. Dispersing them across the town would stretch resources and potentially bring them into conflict with other Friday night revellers. It looked like being a long night and an even longer weekend.

Chapter 30

The screech of sirens, and early season holiday makers hurrying away from the pier entrance told Neil that something was happening at the pub his mates had assembled at. After a long, hot afternoon spent trudging around the town centre, he'd headed to the pier in the hope that Stuart had picked up the message from their mother. With the time approaching 7.15, it now seemed increasingly likely that his brother wasn't planning to arrive in town until match day.

'We're Leeds.United. We'll never be defeated,' was accompanied by the sound of smashing glass as Neil reached the underpass leading from the pier to the pub, just in time to see the first wave of baton wielding riot police charge into the beer garden, followed by red faced officers in shirt sleeves and traditional helmets. The Leeds fans retreated through the smashed doors of the bar and along a pedestrian walkway leading to the main road, whilst repelling the police charge with a hail of bottles and glasses.

A brief stand-off at the doors of the pub between bare chested youths brandishing chairs and bottles and riot police clutching shields and batons, was brought to a sudden end when a dozen officers were chased back down the walkway by a bouncing horde of Leeds fans. It was clear that the drunken jubilance of the afternoon had been replaced by an angrier, more aggressive mood. Neil spotted Hursty dragging Young Sutcliffe back as he swang wild punches at the line of police, and headed up the slope towards them.

"A lad's been knocked over at the top of the ramp. Looks really bad." Hursty still managed to look shell shocked after five hours of sustained drinking.

"Fucking law killed him. Chased him into' road!" Young Sutcliffe's face was sunburnt purple and his eyes bulged excitedly at the prospect of imminent violence.

"They started it, let's fucking give 'em it. Come on Leeds!" Sutcliffe was at the front, as fifty youths charged down the walkway, straight into a barrage of truncheons. Neil and Hursty began to back-up towards the road, only to be overtaken by lads sprinting past with shirts spattered in blood, and a mob of jogging riot police close behind.

On the main road, a crowd had gathered around a body lying on the tarmac, around ten feet in front of a Talbot Horizon with a smashed windscreen. A youth in his late teens in a Union Jack cricket-hat sat on the kerb, shaking his head, clearly distraught, as an ambulance arrived and began to pick its way through the crowd in the road.

"He's dead mate. Fucking brains all over' road." A bare chested kid with long curly hair shook his head as he emerged from the crowd.

"Coppers have killed a Leeds fan," was the shouted verdict as others began to make their way from the destroyed pub.

"Jesus. It's really going to kick off now." Neil had had less to drink than most and could almost sense the powder keg which was about to blow.

"Come on let's see if we can get in a pub before most of this lot get there. I can see it being carnage when they do." Neil and Hursty glanced towards the grim faced paramedics doing their work on the injured Leeds fan and headed towards Bournemouth town centre.

Chapter 31

Roger Thorpe had expected to spend his Friday night drinking gin and tonic at Highcliffe Sailing Club after an exhilarating afternoon out on the water. He should have been smiling politely at Keith's frankly awful jokes and brushing Carol's hand away, as she playfully patted his head and told him he should have warn a cap in the sun.

Instead, he was pacing the control room at the central police station in Madeira Road, sticky with sweat and stale beer and a bottle shaped bruise throbbing on his shoulder. On his second packet of Rothmans of the night, sipping shit coffee in the radio room and eight year old single malt in his office.

He'd explained to Morgan that there was no point in him being on the streets. He needed to be at the heart of the nerve centre, where he could take control of operations. The incident with the Leeds fan on Bath Road had led to a rapid deterioration in the situation. Thankfully, the hooligan had regained consciousness and was currently classed as stable in the Royal. That hadn't stopped rumours spreading through the town that he'd died. Morgan kept asking for an update on his condition because the West Yorkshire 'intelligence' thought it would help 'diffuse' the situation. Fuck them. Fuck them all. Let them think he's dead. They'll respect us more.

Roger Thorpe had never used the new computerised system which allowed him to listen to live radio communications from his office, but as the evening progressed, the scotch became considerably more appealing than the machine coffee and he made his excuses to the chattering gathering of officers in the control room and headed for the sanctuary of his office on the 4th floor.

Janet turned on the machine and tapped the keys until a disembodied voice crackled through the speaker. Thorpe told Janet he could manage now, retrieved the bottle of whiskey from a drawer, locked the office door and closed the blinds. He then turned off the light, lit a cigarette and listened as his town burnt.

'Serious disturbance, Bourne Avenue.'

'Large group of men fighting, corner of Exeter Road and Terrace Road.'

'Urgent assistance, Poet's Corner pub. Windows smashed, officers under attack.'

Fucking intelligence. Fuck you all.

'Shop windows smashed, Poole Hill. Looting in progress.'

'Bouncers attacked, windows smashed, Chablis bar.'

Should have been sailing. Gin and Tonics.

'Ocean Palace Chinese Restaurant, Priory Road. Two waiters thrown through a window in an argument about someone singing.'

'Criterion Bar, Old Christchurch Road under attack by a mob of fifty Leeds supporters.'

Bastards. He and Carol had their first date at the Criterion.

'Car on fire; assault; windows smashed; car overturned; assault; large scale disorder; officers need assistance; assault; Bachus bar, Pumphrey's, Zig Zags...urgent assistance required.'

Fuck you, drunken northern scum and your fucking polo shirts and trainers and intelligence in your car boot. Career coppers. Politician's PACE lapdogs. Fuck you all. Roger Thorpe pulled the phone across his desk and lifted the receiver, waiting for the buzz.

Ring. Ring. Ring. Ring. Ring. Ring. Ten to midnight. Fuck you. Ring. Ring. Ring.

A muffled voice, surprised, disturbed.

"Hello?"

"Chief Constable? It's Roger Thorpe. Bournemouth is under attack. I need urgent assistance."

"What...what time is it?"

"Almost midnight and I'm sorry to disturb you sir..." Roger Thorpe drank a slug of whiskey and smiled.

"...But I'm afraid to say that our intelligence seems to have failed us. My town is currently being besieged by thousands of hooligans and we're very close to losing control. I'm calling to officially inform you that without reinforcements I can't guarantee the safety of the public or my officers if tomorrow's game goes ahead."

Roger Thorpe stayed quiet, relishing the pause and audible sigh he barely detected down the line.

"Leave it with me Roger. Don't worry, we won't abandon you."

Roger Thorpe replaced the receiver, put out his cigarette, tilted his chair and closed his eyes. Tonight he'd dream of bare chests and broken bodies, flying beer bottles, screeching sirens and smashed glass. Tomorrow he'd get his revenge. Fuck you all.

Chapter 32

Saturday 5 May 1990

Drunken Fans on Rampage-- Running Battles with Riot Police-- Leeds United fans clashed with ranks of police in riot gear on the eve of United's promotion decider in Bournemouth. Hundreds of chanting thugs, many wearing 'Bournemouth Invasion 90' T-shirts were involved in a sickening orgy of violence and destruction in the seaside town. Between two and five thousand fans are estimated to be in the town without tickets, with many camping on the beach or in vans and cars in beachfront car parks.

Max Jackson woke with a start and instinctively reached for the Glock under his pillow. Blinded by a light shining in his face, he blinked his red eyes open and sat up.

A shaft of dawn sunlight lit up the room through the opened curtains, and a silhouetted figure stood, arms outstretched and casting a long shadow on the far wall.

"Boss? What the fuck...what time is it?" Max squinted at the Tag Heuer Pilot on the bedside table. 4.10am.

"Listen!" Connolly turned, naked, arms spread wide, in crucifixion pose.

"Boss, what? It's four in the morning. Where have you been?"

Connolly raised both index fingers and tilted his head.

"Can you hear the dolphins Maxie? Can you hear them?"

"They're not dolphins gaffer, they're seagulls." Max pulled the pillow over his head and tensed as he felt Connolly sit on the end of his bed and begin to pat his lower legs as he started to recount the night's events.

Alan Connolly had enjoyed his night at the seaside. A few pints then a Chinese meal at a restaurant in town. Then they'd wheeled out their new sing-a-long machine. It even displayed the lyrics to the songs on a screen with a bouncing arrow to guide you along. Not that Connolly needed that. Only five Stones songs on the machine and obviously he knew all the words anyway. He'd blown them all away. Cheering and applause. They'd loved him. Then some pissed-up lassies had started complaining when he'd begun Satisfaction for the third time. Wanted to have a go at Gloria fucking Gaynor, for Christ's sake. Some wee chink had tried to grab the microphone and it had all got a bit out of hand. Non-Stop Nigel had put them straight though. Connolly was still knocking out Sympathy for the Devil when the law turned up, followed by the ambulances.

Into a taxi with a few of the Asylum lads to some shite disco in an industrial estate somewhere off the M27. Market Dave had stuck two small pieces of paper to his tongue on the way, and by the time they got there he hadn't minded the drug addicts in smiley t-shirts waving their arms about with their mouths wide open. The songs sounded like the needle was stuck and the kid playing the tunes had laughed when he'd asked for the Stones. Normally, Connolly would have reached into his jacket and that kid would have been smiling wider than he ever had, but suddenly it hadn't seemed worth the effort.

Eventually he'd heard the sound of the sea above the shit music and set off walking to the beach. Picked up on the motorway hard shoulder by a shop fitter from

Dorchester, he'd followed the sound of the crashing waves until his espadrilles crunched through blood and glass and he'd watched the sun rise from the end of the pier.

And now, sitting on Max's bed with the sun streaming into the room he could hear the dolphins singing, and he could actually see the sound waves dancing around the room. Catching them on his fingers, changing their direction, weaving patterns of colour and light. Dolphin music. An orchestra of whales and he was the conductor. In control of the sea and all it's creatures. Feeling powerful. Taking control.

"No prisoners today brother." Keith danced before him in the shifting light and his skin was blue, almost translucent, and his eyes were deep and black.

"Gaffer, you need to get some sleep. Big job today remember?"

"Aye son? What's the plan then?" Connolly flicked his hand and the sound waves spread across the room like dispersed smoke.

Max shook his head. For fuck's sake.

"It's your plan remember? We take the mini-bus to the stadium late morning and wait. When the kid shows up we grab him, bag him up and drive him to the New Forest. Make him take us to the cash. Then get rid of him."

"No prisoners right son?"

"That's what you said boss." Max watched from his pillow as Alan Connolly prowled naked in the dawn sunlight, bayonet in hand, slashing and jabbing at the sound waves which swirled about him like a brightly coloured mist. The fog lifting. Killing the snakes. Taking control.

"I don't need to sleep Max. I can see everything more clearly now. Today will be a great day. I can feel it."

Chapter 33

Neil Yardsley shivered as the sun appeared slowly above an apartment block high on the grassy headland to his left. He groaned and shook sand from his shirt as he sat up and checked his watch. 5.10am. A non-stop stream of pissed-up, speeding, tripping, blood soaked, late night story-tellers had been bad enough. Then three lads from Batley had rapped on the van doors at 4am selling Armani jumpers they'd snagged through the smashed-in shutters of Cecil Gee. That was the final straw and Neil had taken himself to the beach, dug himself a narrow trench and attempted to grab a couple of hours sleep.

Now he cast a wary eye along the beach towards the thirty or so other lads who'd had the same idea, as he scrabbled in the sand to retrieve a supermarket carrier bag. He felt the reassuring weight of the pistol. His insurance policy if thinks went seriously pear-shaped.

Seeing no signs of life at the van, he headed to town and edged into McDonalds past a team of red eyed glaziers who'd had the busiest night of their lives. Three plate glass windows destroyed wasn't going to stop the relentless urge of the world's favourite corporate clown to make money, and Neil was able to sit down to a breakfast McMuffin, conscious of the gun shaped bulge tucked into the back of his jeans beneath his t-shirt. Hopefully he'd be able to intercept Stu at Dean Court before Connolly got to him and stash the gun before going into the ground.

By 7am McDonalds was already filling with rough-sleeping Leeds fans and the snippets of conversation painted a picture of a night Bournemouth was unlikely to forget.

"...five bouncers, big blokes with baseball bats, they didn't stand a chance. Must have been forty Leeds..."

"...The coppers were running, took their helmets off and threw them away, one of them went down. Got a right hiding..."

"...All' staff left. Ran off. These lads booted the door in. They've got crates of ale. Knocking it out now in that car park..."

"...They're saying there's a special court Monday. He's got' car keys so we're stuck till then."

"...Never seen owt like it mate. Fucking hell."

Neil called into a newsagents on his way back to the van and the Asian shopkeeper and an old woman buying a Daily Mail and a loaf of bread fell silent and shifted uneasily as he entered.

Local radio were devoting most of the news bulletin to the previous night's events and talking about police reinforcements being drafted in from Portsmouth, Southampton and London. The weather, Southern heatwave, Northern showers. Then the first cheesy banter on the early breakfast show. Bruno Brookes and Liz Kershaw. Radio 1. It was national news headlines. Fucking hell.

Back at the van, Young Sutcliffe was brandishing a Marc O'Polo sweatshirt which had been beige at the start of the night but now had a claret back and sleeve. One of his mates was grimacing as he examined a congealed mass of blood below Sutcliffe's crown.

"Those fucking bouncers are going to get it tonight." He rummaged in his bag and retrieved a toothbrush and bottle of water.

"You think owt's going to be open tonight? I reckon it will be a total lockdown." Hursty was trying to remove an unidentified stain from his trainers with a wad of tissue.

"It's made national radio news. Just heard it. Extra coppers coming in from all over." Neil took off his shirt and reclined on the grass verge, feeling the sun start to warm his chilled bones.

"Jesus. National news. Fuck me, we're going to get a right bollocking over this." The fact that they'd made the front pages filtered back to the lads still curled up in sleeping bags in the back of the van.

"Might as well make the most of it then. Let's go out with a bang." Sutcliffe rolled his hundred quid sweatshirt into a ball and stuffed it into an overflowing waste bin.

"Straight through' gates at' ground this afternoon. No way they can stop 5000 of us without tickets. It's going to be mayhem."

Neil felt the hard form of the gun pressing into the small of his back. Let's go out with a bang. It's going to be mayhem.

Chapter 34

Julie Statham had felt like she'd landed in a war zone when she'd pulled her Corsa off the dual carriageway near Bournemouth station at 2am. Blue lights and sirens; groups of officers in riot gear; flashing orange lights and fat glaziers in hi-vis vests; groups of staggering men in knee-length shorts and baggy tops. Roads blocked by police vehicles or strewn with debris had sent her back the way she'd come, to the comparative calm of Christchurch, where she'd parked near the harbour. Exhausted after the longest drive of her life, in which she'd had too much time to think, she'd fallen asleep immediately.

A 4am sunrise had flooded the car with harsh light and Julie had spent two hours in the reclined passenger seat, staring at the ceiling, wondering where Richard was, what he'd done and who he was hiding from. Then she'd picked at a bacon rind sandwich washed down with a milky instant coffee in an early opening café.

"You from up North then? Down for the match?" The middle aged woman serving was friendly enough, but Julie wasn't in the mood for conversation.

"No, just visiting someone."

"You be careful then. Apparently those Leeds fans have just about destroyed Bournemouth already. Been on the radio. Terrible it is. I'd steer well clear if I were you."

Three hours later and Julie was wishing she'd heeded the waitress's advice. The tension in Bournemouth was evident when she'd squeezed her car between a Salford rental van and a transit bearing a Wakefield phone number. Large groups of men occupied the car park, kicking footballs or lounging in the sun. Car stereos pumped out an eclectic early morning mix of Bridewell Taxis, 808 State and Ronnie Hilton. Bare chests and Leeds shirts. Gateways supermarket bags bulging with cans and bottles. 10am felt like 10pm.

Across the road, lines of police vans, Belfast style metal grills fixed to windscreens for the first time ever in Dorset. Side doors open, the occupants sweating in helmets and body armour. Watching, waiting, hating. Today they'd get their revenge.

Clutching a folded photo that Christine had given her, Julie made her way along the seafront. She'd only met Neil once. She thought she'd recognise him but wasn't sure. She'd never seen Stuart. The photo was five years old. Two brothers, grinning, clutching bottles of Budweiser, Stuart's head tilted in response to his brother's playful headlock. Eyes burning flash red. Five years ago. Before jail terms and lung disease. Underworld graft and bags of cash. Madchester and Acid house. Sergeant Wilko and Vinnie Jones. Before a new decade and the end of the 80's.

Julie felt conspicuous and vulnerable walking through the crowds of Leeds fans on the seafront, sandals sticking to last night's beer and crunching on broken glass. At least she'd chosen a yellow summer top and dark skirt when she'd thrown some clothes into a bag and jumped in the car. She cringed at the thought that she could have easily chosen the new red summer dress she'd bought from Principles - definitely the wrong colour for this weekend. Past the pier displaying a huge Union Jack with Retford Whites in large painted letters, down the slope towards the beach, hoping for less attention here.

She heard a large cheer as soon as she kicked off her sandals, sand too hot for her feet already, and hoped it wasn't directed at her. She looked towards the horizon and headed for the shoreline.

'Get your tits out, get your tits out...' the chant started from behind her and normally she'd turn to confront the little boys and their infantile songs, but not today. The whole town felt dangerous, out of control.

'Get your tits out for the lads...' Julie felt her face redden and carried on staring forward as she walked through crowds of lads drinking, laughing and thrusting their hips in her direction.

She cursed her own naivety in thinking she'd arrive in a small seaside resort and easily locate Neil amongst a handful of Leeds fans drinking quietly in a seafront bar. Calmly explain why she was there and help the poor guy deal with the news. Then go meet his brother and help him sort out the mess he was in. Instead, she'd walked into a dangerously lawless situation which seemed to be bordering on anarchy. The nearest police were a few hundred yards away in front of the pier, it was unlikely they'd hear her cries for help and even if they did, the beach felt like a no-go zone for the law.

Julie tried to block out the crude comments and chants but became aware of a persistent voice over her shoulder.

"Where you going love? Are you lost?" She ignored him at first, but he broke into a jog and appeared alongside her. Bare chested, Leeds Yorkshire Rose tattoo over his heart, baseball cap back to front, can of lager in his hand and a friendly smile.

"Do you live here love? It's not a great day for a stroll on the beach."

"No, I'm from Leeds. I've lost my boyfriend." The lad's demeanour altered upon hearing her accent and his smile changed to an expression of concern.

"You really don't want to be wandering round here on your own love, let me walk you back to the road."

Julie nodded and her chaperone raised two fingers and shouted fuck off to his mates who'd begun cheering and chanting 'he's a rapist.'

"Try and find your chap love. You don't want to be wandering around on your own. It's going to really kick off in the next couple of hours." The lad waved her off near the pier and jogged back to his mates.

Julie headed up into the town centre, past boarded up pubs and shops, and the handful of Saturday shoppers who cast a wary eye towards the small groups of Leeds fans loitering around, trying in vain to find a drink. She found a Littlewoods store and headed to the café. Finding Neil at the stadium seemed like a long shot but she had to give it a go. Failing that, the potential 7pm meeting at the pier was the only chance she'd get to catch him, although there was a good chance that would be too late. For all she knew, the deadly collision between Neil, Stuart and Connolly might have already happened.

Julie sipped her tea and nibbled half-heartedly at a scone, listening to pensioners picking at their triangle sandwiches while clucking and shaking their heads, discussing the hooligan invasion. She'd hoped the long drive would help clear he head, let her think more clearly but it had only made things worse. 250 miles from home, in a strange town, sleeping in her car, with a missing husband and a murdered cat, the truth was that Julie Statham had never felt more alone in her life.

Chapter 35

"Fuck, how hot is it in here? I'm melting man..." Evrol mopped his dripping forehead with an already soaked T-shirt as he slumped in the back of the mini bus.

"Can't we turn the engine on again Max? Get some air blowing through..."

"Too many coppers around lads. We'll attract attention." Max hung his head through the driver's side window and watched the ranks of police in shirt sleeves and riot helmets taking up position in the scrubby sand car park at Dean Court stadium.

"We'll attract attention? When Don Johnson is wandering about with a fucking bayonet in his jacket talking to his imaginary brother?" Evrol and Steve exchanged glances and shook their heads. Even Non-Stop Nigel puffed out his cheeks and for a brief second it seemed even he might break his customary silence to complain. Instead, he mopped his brow and watched the lines of riot police assembling through the van window.

Connolly seemed oblivious to the massed ranks of the law surrounding him as he flitted around the car park, soaking up the atmosphere. Chatting to Leeds fans, promising everyone tickets, laughing with the nervous looking stewards, joking with the police, jigging along to the chants of the first ticketless arrivals.

He'd slept in a chair for a couple of hours, then burst into the bathroom while Max was on the bog and taken a cold shower without speaking. Then the lads had eaten breakfast whilst watching him pacing the terrace, looking towards the distant sea while engaged in a heated debate with an unseen companion.

Then in the mini-bus to the ground when Max had loaded up the usual Stones cassette, Connolly had shaken his head and turned it off, saying he wanted to listen.

"To what?" Max had asked, and his boss had smiled and chuckled and wound down the window, and run his fingers along the length of the bayonet in his jacket pocket.

"He's really fucking weird today. We need to watch him." Steve sat with his legs out of the side door of the bus as Connolly embraced an old man decked out in a Union Jack suit and top hat.

"Just keep an eye out for the kid. The sooner we grab him, the sooner we can get out of here. All these coppers are scaring the shit out of me." Max shuffled his feet and pushed the Glock further under his seat as Connolly turned and waved, grinning manically, now sporting a cream suit and wearing a Union Jack top hat.

Chapter 36

The tabloids on sale at WH Smiths at Waterloo had gone to print too early to report on the previous evening's events, and Stuart had spent Friday night at Daisy Chain at the Brixton Fridge, so had missed the late news bulletins carrying the first reports from Bournemouth. The conversation of four Cockney Whites in his carriage on the 10.35 to the south coast provided the first clue that the day was going to be as lively as he'd expected. They'd had a phone call from mates already in the town and been told to stock up on beer in London.

"Town's locked down mate. Pubs and off licences all shut. No chance of a drink." Stuart didn't mind too much after only four hours sleep and a night on the doves. He just hoped Danno hadn't been nicked last night with their tickets. Knowing him though he'd probably found an underground techno club and was totally unaware that anything had even kicked off.

Stuart realised how unlikely that was as soon as he walked out of Bournemouth station and saw the lines of police vans and scowling officers in full riot gear. It was clear that everyone in Bournemouth was fully aware of the previous night's events and knew there was more of the same to come. The forty or so Leeds fans from the train were searched and stripped of alcohol, then directed to the left, past the barking dogs and piles of horse shit. Then another row of vans at the end of the road turned them left again.

"They obviously don't want us in town or on the seafront. Bet it's kicking off down there already." A bloke in a yellow Top Man shirt with a southern accent grimaced at the thought of a beerless day. "I knew we should have come yesterday."

"Yeah same here." Stuart agreed. A night clubbing in Brixton had seemed more appealing than a night trashing seaside pubs with pissed up Leeds fans, but a nagging doubt was now forming in his mind that Danno might not be waiting for him at the turnstile at 2pm.

Chapter 37

The smell of his own breath almost made Roger Thorpe retch. A full night of Rothmans and Scotch always tasted terrible the next morning, but after four hours snatched sleep in his office chair and a quick mouth swill with no toothpaste, it was no wonder the two constables in the Dean Court control box were giving their superior officer a wide berth.

The morning roll call had confirmed that the Chief Constable hadn't let him down. Eighty lads from Southampton. Sixty eight from Pompey. Forty from the Met including a 16 strong TSG squad who normally spent their time bashing the blacks in South London. Plus Dorset at full strength, all leave cancelled. Pumped up on time and a half, all eager to crack some Yorkshire skulls. Today was his day. A day for revenge. Fuck you all.

No problems with the pubs. Those with intact windows knew they'd been lucky and were boarding up anyway. They'd advised the supermarkets to stay closed or clear the booze shelves, but the greedy bastards had opened anyway and already been cleaned out. He'd told his men to stand down when the calls started coming in at 8.30 saying the beer aisles were being emptied and no one was paying. Money grabbing corporate fools. Fuck them all.

He hadn't needed the West Yorkshire 'intelligence' to know what was coming. They'd positioned themselves by the pier, with their binoculars and cameras. Taking photos and making notes on their risk targets to add to the files in the boot of their car. Worn their polo shirts and trainers, their jeans and sunglasses to blend in. To observe and analyse, theorise and understand. Fuck them.

When the first radio call came in, Roger Thorpe already knew. Already understood their plan, anticipated their next move. How could he not after thirty five years? That's why he was at the stadium, not pissing about on the beach. The stadium was where it would happen.

'Leeds supporters now leaving the seafront en-masse. Heading east on Holdenhurst Road.'

Roger Thorpe lit a cigarette and blew smoke over the flickering blue screen before him.

The buzz of disembodied radio chatter filled the room and the glare from the screen illuminated the darkened, sweat infused room. Bare pink chests and yellow away shirts reflected the bright early afternoon sun, and clouds of dust from the car park gravel made the fast-moving crowds appear like ghostly apparitions on the screen.

'Group of youths approaching the TSG'

"Tell them to maintain their position, don't allow them to pass." Thorpe inhaled deeply on his cigarette, and fought the fatigue that caused his eyelids to close.

"What's going on there? Zoom in on that group." A diminutive figure in a Union Jack suit and top hat, surrounded by bare chests.

'Looks like Ken Bailey sir.' The local eccentric and well known England fan was usually happy to be the centre of attention. Not today, as grinning youths surrounded him and posed for photos, arms raised in Nazi salutes.

'Should we assist sir?'

'Missiles being thrown...missiles being thrown at officers.'

"Give me the radio constable." Roger Thorpe put out his cigarette on the wall and motioned with his hand.

"Move forward...come on, move forward, move forward. Deploy, deploy."

Ranks of blue helmets advanced through the rising dust cloud as the Leeds fans scattered. Those who fell, felt the full force of the Tactical Support Group's batons.

"Excellent." Thorpe smiled and lit another cigarette as he watched a youth curled into a foetal ball being clubbed and stamped on by three officers.

"Hold this view. Hold it here...I'll tell you when to move."

As soon as the TSG advance halted, the Leeds fans were re-grouping, emboldened by increasing numbers.

"There's a charge coming up, there's a charge...hold the line." Thorpe breathed deeply as he saw the police ranks start to retreat.

'Missiles being thrown. Missiles from all directions.' The voice on the radio was almost drowned out by the roar of the charging Leeds fans.

"Come on, come on! Dispersal tactics... dispersal tactics again."

A youth in an orange t-shirt and a white bucket hat launched a flying drop kick at the lead officer as the police line advanced. Then the fans were running again, the blue helmets charging again into the dust cloud. The radio chatter was now obscured by the loud, fenzied barking of a dog.

"There's movement to the right of the TSG unit. Missiles being thrown from the right."

Thorpe lit another cigarette as he watched forty youths, arms outstretched, beckoning, goading, urging the police to advance. The radio now crackled with a flood of incoherent and increasingly panicked communications.

'On the right, outflanking TSG...'

'Rushing individually... they're going to rush as a unit....'

'WILL YOU MOVE BACK PLEASE...'

'There's a unit near the road, come back into the main body of police officers, this could be a trap...'

'We are Leeds, We are Leeds, We are Leeds...'

'1314 West Yorkshire... your units are going onto the car park, they're getting sucked in. They're coming from the back, you want them near the cars...'

Roger Thorpe's eyes narrowed at the sound of the flat Yorkshire vowels.

"Officer. Officer. OFFICER."

No response. Only louder barking and We are Leeds.

"This is Gold Command, come in please."

'Received Gold Command.'

"Who's that?"

'PC Mason sir.'

"Get that West Yorkshire officer back on this channel."

The camera panned across the crowds at the far end of the car park, standing beneath the trees. A blur of bodies in the haze, occasional arms extended from within the crowd, hurling missiles.

"1314 West Yorkshire, Sergeant Barton, over."

"Sergeant, this is Gold Command, over."

The radio crackled with the sound of cheering and a cacophony of barking.

"This is Gold Command, are you there sergeant?"

'Missiles from the rear...unit on the right forced to retreat...we can't cope with these numbers...missiles from the front.'

"This is Gold..."

"They've got them isolated now, they've seen how many they are...there's a charge, there's a charge, they're going to get overwhelmed."

"This is Gold Command over, do you read me 1314 West Yorkshire?"

"Sir...Sergeant Barton, West Yorkshire. Your lads are getting sucked in. They need to get back closer to the ground. Get the lads back to the ground with the horses, keep us all together, they're all disorientated."

Hundreds now, running at speed across the car park, a hail of missiles raining down on the retreating police lines.

"I'm well aware of what's happening Sergeant. I'm monitoring the whole situation. It's under control."

Incessant chatter on the radio, unintelligible through the roar of the crowd and the static. A youth in a blue t-shirt filling the screen, throwing, crouching, throwing, crouching. The camera panned out to reveal dozens of others adopting the same stance.

"Can't we get this fucking picture any clearer? I can't see what's going on."

"I'm sorry sir, it's the glare and the dust. Makes it impossible to focus."

"Fucking useless." Roger Thorpe lit another cigarette and wished he had his hip flask. Four horses cantered onto the screen from the right, scattering the stone throwers in all directions.

'I tell you what, you can't doubt the coppers bravery can you? They're surrounded there look. Look they're all around them. Bloody brave.'

"Who the fuck is that?"

"No idea sir, sounded local though. Wonder if an officer has lost their radio."

"Jesus Christ, that's all we need."

The Leeds fans getting bolder now. A youth in a white baseball cap and black t-shirt with a green logo, leading the advance, brandishing a large piece of wood. Others behind, running, throwing, crouching to pick up stones, running throwing, crouching.

'Who's in charge here?' The Yorkshire accent again.

"I'm in charge sergeant, I'm the Gold commander." Roger Thorpe leant towards the screen and exhaled smoke, causing the constable at the monitor to cough.

'Who's in charge? You need to get your lads behind the horses, they're getting dragged in and isolated.'

"I'm in charge Sergeant! I'm in charge." Thorpe clicked the transmitter switch on the radio. "Is this bloody thing working?"

"I don't think he's talking to you sir."

'Get your lads back. Mop up after the horses. This is fucking chaos and we're losing control.'

"Sergeant, stand down. This isn't a West Yorkshire operation. I'm in charge. I'm the Gold commander. Why are those officers retreating?"

'Mounted units for dispersal then the troops on foot can mop up. That's it lads, pull back. Pull back.'

"Dorset units, do not pull back. This is Chief Inspector Thorpe. Gold Commander. Do not withdraw, that's an order."

The Leeds fans advanced again, running, throwing, crouching as the police retreated, shields raised against the hail of missiles raining down on them.

"Dorset and Hampshire units, are you receiving? Advance towards the main body of supporters. Do not retreat. I repeat, do not retreat. This is Gold commander, and I'm in charge here."

We are Leeds, we are Leeds, interrupted by six horses galloping into a fleeing crowd, batons swinging, bodies tumbling beneath flying hooves.

The static buzz of the radio interrupted again by the flat vowels of the North.

'No one's in charge here. We've fucking lost control and if we don't do something about it, someone's going to get killed.'

Roger Thorpe put another cigarette out on the wall and stared, unseeing, into the distorted glare of the monitor screen. Shouldn't even be here. Should have been sailing. Thirty five years. Eight months from retirement. Fuck you. Fuck you all.

Chapter 38

The dust stung Neil's eyes and caused him to choke as he stood on a small wall to try and locate a route through the mayhem. Lads beside him wrapped t-shirts around their faces as protection against the sun's heat and the clouds of dust being thrown up by the hooves of the horses charging into the car park crowds. A surge of red faced, wild eyed fans surged towards Neil, panicked by a loose horse stampeding towards them, dragging its rider alongside as he struggled to free his feet from the stirrups.

The front line of the battle was shifting in waves. The Leeds fans, bouncing on their toes, edging forward, beckoning, goading. The leaders clutching handfuls of stones and others brandishing lumps of wood and red and white accident cones. Getting braver as they saw the hesitation in the police ranks. Emboldened by a roar from their rear, a charge forward, covered by a hail of missiles from those on the periphery.

The police backed off until there was no way to go, or until their radios told them that colleagues were isolated and cornered by the mob. Then the mounted section advanced first, the thunder of hooves causing panic in the Leeds fans who turned and ran. The infantry followed close behind, batons drawn and Perspex shields rattling under a drum-beat of hurled rocks as they broke their line and followed the horses, cracking skulls and ribs.

Neil pushed through crowds of families and older supporters huddled for safety beneath the small main stand, towards a line of officers guarding the turnstiles and reached the open end which would house the 2000 Leeds fans lucky enough to have a ticket. It was clear that the cordon designed to repel ticketless fans hadn't worked due to the large number of forgeries, and angry fans brandished tickets at a line of impassive officers, helmet visors rendering them deaf to the protests.

"They're saying the ground's already full. This is fucking ridiculous. I haven't missed a game since 1976!" the face of a balding forty-something was streaked with tears or sweat or both.

Years of arriving at grounds without tickets had served Neil well, and he quickly moved away from the main throng of supporters pushing at the police line, to the far side of the cordon. Watching, waiting until he saw his chance. A family group with a sobbing girl in a wheelchair, father looking shellshocked, mother calming a ginger ten year old in a Leeds away shirt. A brief conversation and the police line parted to admit them, an elderly couple in matching yellow sun hats also shuffled forward, with Neil close behind, waving his ticket at an officer who was now arguing with a fan a few feet to the right.

Now within the cordon, in position next to the turnstile, gun hidden in his jeans, Neil scanned the crowd. 1.45. All he had to do now was spot his brother.

Chapter 39

The walk from the station to Dean Court was a struggle in 90° heat after four hours sleep, and Stuart stopped at a Shell garage and was queuing, holding a sandwich and bottle of coke when a police van with blue lights flashing pulled onto the forecourt. A group of officers in shirt sleeves and blue riot helmets disembarked and one waved to catch the attendant's attention, then gave him a throat cutting gesture.

The plump Asian stopped serving and shrugged, prompting the officer to shake his head and hurry to the door.

"You need to close."

"What? Close?" It was clear the attendant wasn't aware that his town was now on a war footing.

"There are five hundred Leeds fans heading up Holdenhurst Road now to try and force their way into Dean Court. We can't guarantee your safety if you stay open. I'd pull the shutters down if I were you." He turned and left, leaving the Asian open mouthed and shaking his head.

The queue quickly dispersed with motorists thrusting cash over the counter and hurrying to get their cars out of the firing line. Stuart sat on a low wall and opened his sandwich wrapper. Hopefully Danno might be with the main body of Leeds fans advancing on the ground. Rumours were circulating that the police were going to prevent anyone without a ticket getting close to the stadium, which would make his planned turnstile meeting difficult.

It didn't take long to work out that spotting Danno was going to be an almost impossible task. An advance guard of barechested, jogging fans was closely followed by a vast mob, who announced their presence via a distant 'We are Leeds' chant a few minutes before they appeared, marching like an army along the main road. A handful of drivers unlucky enough to have chosen that particular time on this specific day to drive towards the town centre, screeched to an abrupt halt and began to execute rapid three-point-turns as their vehicles were quickly surrounded by the fast moving wave of Leeds fans.

Shirts off, bottles and cans in hand, battle anthems in full cry, the Leeds fans brushed aside a half-hearted police attempt to contain them, and marched on towards Bournemouth's tiny ground. Stuart swigged off the last off his coke, tossed the bottle into a bus stop bin and fell in with the main body of fans. If he couldn't find Danno, he'd need to make sure he was at the front when they stormed the gates, which now seemed highly likely.

Looking around, Stuart spotted familiar faces - flushed with the heat and twenty-four hours of drinking, excited at the prospect of renewing the previous night's hostilities with the police. Only this time it wasn't going to be Dorset plod, today it would be the A team of Hampshire plus the Met's Tactical Support Group.

Stuart's first view of the ground was obscured by a haze of chalky dust drifting on the breeze from a large gravel car park on the right, flanked by tall trees. The smashed windscreens and dented roofs and bonnets of parked vehicles told a tale of earlier disorder. It felt like the arrival of the latest wave of Leeds fans had interrupted a break in the riot, and officers swigging from bottles with their helmets removed were quickly marshalled into lines to deal with this new influx of fans, who wasted no time in charging the cordon surrounding the Leeds turnstiles.

Blinking in the harsh glare, Stuart joined other fans standing on a small wall, who were watching sporadic hand-to-hand skirmishes breaking out across the car park. Stuart's focus was on the area around the Leeds end, and he scanned the milling crowds, searching for Danno's familiar grinning face. He needed to be closer, so jumped off the wall and shoved his way through the crowds, his eyes fixed on those hanging around within the police cordon, no doubt like Danno trying to locate friends and family to hand over tickets.

His gaze settled on a heavily tattooed man with a shaved head and crimson sunburnt back, who was engaged in a shoving match with an officer in the police line. The outcome was predictable, and he was smashed in the face with a police shield before three officers pinned him face down to the gravel. As the police line broke, a familiar face appeared in Stuart's line of sight.

"Neil...what the fuck?" Stuart's brother was about fifty yards away and waving frantically towards him. Stuart began to smile and was about to wave back when he caught the panicked expression on Neil's face. Shaking his head, mouthing no...go...trying to get out of the cordon but being pushed back by the police, waving his arms, pointing away from the ground.

"I'm meeting Danno." Stuart tried to shout above the sound of chants and screams, but Neil couldn't hear, waving his arms and shaking his head. A red and white police cone sailed through the dust to hit a galloping mounted officer squarely in the chest and propelled him backwards to a huge cheer. Panicked, his horse bucked and reared, then charged towards the crowd, where two mid-twenties black men were jogging forward. Stuart turned back towards Neil, then froze. Two mid-twenties black men. He looked again in time to see them swerve to avoid being trampled, then carry on running in his direction. Two mid-twenties black men. Evrol and Steve. And behind them, the lumbering figure of Non-Stop Nigel, confused and stumbling amidst the melee.

The appearance of his brother and Connolly's gang afflicted Stuart with a split second of paralysis, but as soon as the adrenaline kicked in, he was off. Sprinting through the crowd, barging slow moving fans out of the way, breathless from sucking dust and with his heart pounding, Stuart was soon away from the ground and running back towards town, checking over his shoulder every few seconds, with his mind racing.

A car horn sounding as it passed made him jump, and the little green Corsa pulled up ahead. Stuart paused, about to flee down a sidestreet, until he saw the driver was a young woman. She opened the door and got out. Dark hair, glasses, yellow top and black skirt. Like a primary school teacher.

"Stuart? Are you Stuart Yardsley?" Holding a picture. A picture of him and Neil.

"I'm Julie, your mum's friend. I thought it was you when I saw you running out of the car park. I saw the men chasing after you. Quick, get in, we need to get away from here right now."

"But my brother...he's at the ground. I'm meant to meet my mate."

"I don't know exactly what's going on, but I think your Neil does. I need to talk to him too but it's too dangerous to go back there now. I think I know where we can meet him. Come on get in..."

Chapter 40

"What the fuck just happened? We had him, then he took off running..." Max jogged up alongside Steve and Evrol while flinching at the battle raging around him.

"These fucking horses are shitting me up man."

"We were twenty feet away, he was heading right towards us then he just took off," Evrol was looking nervously towards a gang of lads in white KKK hoods who seemed to be paying him a bit too much attention.

"Fuck me... Evrol look!" Steve pointed across the police cordon to a tall man in his mid-twenties wearing a white t-shirt.

"Isn't that the same guy from outside the lads' flat? The bloke who said he was looking for his friend."

The three of them watched as the obviously agitated young man scanned the crowd in the direction Stuart had fled, as Alan Connolly appeared with Non-Stop Nigel.

"I love the smell of napalm in the morning boys! Fuck me this is better than Paris. Now explain to me what just happened."

"We as good as had him boss, then he got spooked and ran. See that lad in the white t-shirt over near the turnstile? We reckon he warned him off somehow."

"For fucks sake boys. He won't be coming back here now. If you're right though, the laddie there is bound to be meeting the kid. You're going to have to stick to him like glue and hope he leads yus to him. Then when you find the boy, ring me at the hotel. Here's some tickets for the match." Connolly peeled off four tickets, all with the same number, from a bundle in his pocket.

"Boss, you're not asking us to go in there?" Steve and Evrol were exchanging nervous glances.

"Like fucking rocking horse shite those tickets you ungrateful cunt, what's the matter with you?"

"Look around boss, we're the only black lads here and there's blokes dressed as the KKK and Adolf Hitler. We could get lynched in there."

"He's right boss. We need to keep a low profile in the ground. Me and Non-Stop will go in and keep an eye on him." Max winked at Steve.

"Okay Maxie. And you two boys can take me back in the mini-bus. It's an afternoon in the pool and the sauna for me, I feel like I need a lie down. And Max..."

"Boss?"

"Don't fucking lose him or you're into me for twenty five large, understand? Good boy. Enjoy the game lads!"

Chapter 41

'United are back, United are back, hello!"

The chant had morphed into a crescendo of emotion as fans poured over the barriers from every side of the pitch at the sound of the final whistle, to join in a jubilant, sun baked, drunken, blood soaked celebration.

Even Max had found himself bouncing around the away terrace in the sweaty embrace of total strangers celebrating Lee Chapman's 50th minute winner, as a deadpan Non-Stop Nigel cuffed away anyone attempting to give him a hug.

Neil had managed to find Hursty in the ground and had joined him and the rest of the lads in saluting the new champions as they appeared in the Dean Court directors' box to celebrate promotion. It had been a long time coming but Neil's mind was elsewhere. Hopefully Stuart had understood his shouted warning and had managed to get out of town. If not, that he'd call home and pick up the message to meet at the pier, so Neil could tell him about Danno and that he needed to pay Connolly back or disappear forever.

Heading back to town, all the talk was of getting some beer for a party on the beach.

"Poole or Christchurch are your best bets. You've no chance here. We've all been told to close," shouted a nervous looking Sikh from the window above his shuttered store.

"Beer-run in a taxi it is then. Tenner each lads and we'll fill up the boot." Hursty held out his hand as his friends fumbled in their pockets.

"I'll see you on the beach later lads, I need to go and meet our kid." Neil waved his mates goodbye and headed towards town with a shouted warning from Young Sutcliffe as a send-off.

"Watch yourself mate. Coppers have told us they're going to really give us it tonight. Them and 'bouncers are out for revenge!"

Chapter 42

"Excuse me mate, I need to use the phone. Emergency." Max yanked open the glass door bearing the British Telecom logo and reached in to remove the receiver from the hand of a sunburnt middle-aged holidaymaker.

"But I'm talking to my mother. She's two hundred miles away and had a fall..." The man's voice trailed off as he spotted Non-Stop Nigel looming up over the smaller man's shoulder.

Max took the hotel card from his pocket and punched in the number while holding the phone box door ajar. The aroma of piss and cigarette smoke was never welcome, but on a day when the glass box on Bournemouth seafront had been subjected to ten hours of 80° sunlight, fresh air was a necessity.

"Good afternoon, High Cliff Hotel." Max recognised the clipped tones of the blonde girl behind reception. If they got this business sorted quickly, he might try his luck there later.

"Afternoon love, could you put me through to Mr. Bremner in Room 62?" Connolly's attempts at hiding his identity were never the most original.

"Maxie...what do you know? Good result today eh? On and off the pitch, so I hear..."

"Yes boss, it was bloody hot though. Non-Stop has lost about two stone in weight. Anyway, we've followed the lad from the ground. He headed straight to the pier. I reckon he's told the kid to meet him here. Better get down here sharpish."

"Good work Max, we'll be there in ten minutes. Don't let the wee bastard out of your sight."

Chapter 43

"Come on, drink up, it's nearly 6 o'clock. If your brother is heading to the pier he could be there by now." Julie thought twice about the remnants of her warm lager and lime, then replaced her glass on the table.

Stuart sat opposite her with his head in hands.

"I just can't get my head round any of this. Why was Neil at the ground instead of Danno? If summat bad has happened to him, it's all my fault. And why was Connolly there? Fucking Connolly..." He cringed at his choice of words.

"Sorry for swearing...but Connolly. Neil's real dad. I just can't believe it."

"I know it's a shock, and I don't know what's happened to your friend. It won't be easy, but Neil needs to know about his dad, and it will be better coming from you than me." Julie stood up as Stuart finished his pint.

"I don't know. I was stupid to think I could get away with this. I need to go see Connolly and offer to return his cash. They can't kill me can they, or they'll never find it? I'm not sure about telling Neil he's his dad though. What good will that do?" Stuart tried to convince himself that he was worth more to Connolly alive than dead, but realised his hands were shaking as he put down his empty glass.

Distant chants and a wailing police siren told them that the first Leeds fans had started to arrive back in the town centre.

"It's up to you what you tell your brother, but this isn't going away until you face up to what you've done and try to put it right. Let's go to the pier and hope Neil's there. Then the two of you can try and set up a meeting with Connolly and hopefully convince him to be reasonable.

"Reasonable?" Despite the situation he was in, Stuart couldn't resist a half smile. "He thinks he's Mick Jagger, carries a bayonet in his jacket, talks to his dead brother and enjoys torturing people. 'Reasonable' isn't really a word you associate with Alan Connolly, Julie."

"No but..." Julie turned away and her voice trailed off.

"But what?"

"Maybe if he finds out who Neil is, he's going to be willing to listen to him?"

"You'd think so, if we were dealing with a sane human being, but Connolly certainly isn't sane and calling him human's a bit of a stretch too." Stuart shuddered and quickly dispelled the thought that Neil may have inherited some of his father's personality traits.

It was clear that the dynamics of the previous evening had changed as soon as Julie parked her car in a sidestreet a block back from the seafront. The Dorset police in their shirt sleeves and brand new, ill-fitting riot helmets of Friday night had been replaced by an eager, tooled-up, paramilitary force who were in the mood for violence. On the ten minute walk towards the pier, Julie and Stuart passed a group of a dozen Leeds fans, arms cuffed behind their backs, lying face down in the gutter and surrounded by a group of masked officers, their shoulder numbers ominously removed. Outside the Holiday Revival beer garden, a group of angry supporters attempted to reach their friend who was laying, bleeding heavily from a head wound, only to be repelled by a baton charge from a batallion of yelling, pumped-up officers.

"Jesus. I dread to think what it's going to be like down here in a few hours." Stuart shook his head as he glanced across to the beach, where shirtless Leeds fans brandishing bags of take-out cans were gathering around piles of smashed deckchairs and some beached rowing boats. Approaching the entrance to the pier, Stuart quickened his step, his eyes scanning the gaggles of bystanders to try and spot Neil. Julie was walking a few feet ahead of him when Stuart sensed a sudden presence at his left shoulder and felt the hard edge of the Glock in the small of his back.

"Don't even think about running." He felt Max's breath on his ear and spotted Non-Stop Nigel cutting off his route ahead.

"There's a silencer on the gun. The bullet will cut through your spinal cord, and I'll be away before the law have scraped your crawling body up and nicked you for D&D."

Julie turned just as Evrol took her arm and gave her a gleaming white smile. "Shush sweetheart." He raised a finger to his lips. "Hey, don't I know you?"

"I'm sorry Max, I made a mistake, I've still got the cash and we can sort this..." Stuart's legs had turned to jelly and he struggled to maintain control of his bowels as his captor guided him back towards the main road.

"Too right you made a mistake mate. The gaffer is none-too-pleased with you, as your little pal found out."

"Danno? Oh fuck no, he knew nowt about it. What did you do to him?"

"He won't be going out dancing with you for a while, put it that way. Now shut it and walk." Max prodded the gun into Stuart's lower back and gripped his arm hard as they walked under the Bath Road underpass.

"Nigel, run ahead and tell Steve to get the van ready." Max monitored the movement of the police ranks, but they were too focused on herding newly arrived Leeds fans down towards the beach to notice them.

"Where are we going? Let go of my arm." Julie sounded close to tears and Stuart felt sick at the impact his actions were having on innocent people.

"Please Max, she's just my mam's friend, she's nowt to do with this. You can let her go."

"Up to the boss." Max glanced back towards Evrol and Julie. "I'm sure I know her from somewhere..."

"Stu!!" The shout came from a group of Leeds fans unloading crates of beer from the boot of a taxi on the main road. Stuart glanced across but didn't acknowledge Hursty, though his expression couldn't hide the terror he was feeling.

"Keep fucking walking." Max sounded agitated now and pushed Stuart on.

Even though he was at the wrong end of a thirty hour drinking session, it didn't take long for Hursty to realise something was wrong. He also knew exactly how to rally the troops to action quickly.

"Sutcliffe! Lads! That's Neil's brother...looks like him and his bird are having some problems with a gang of bouncers."

They'd reached the other side of the underpass and Max could see the van with its hazards flashing, on the road alongside the park. Non-Stop Nigel was heading back towards them when he heard the roar.

"Come on you fuckers! Let's have it! Leeds, Leeds, Leeds!"

The underpass acoustics made it sound like they were being pursued by an army. In reality, it was twenty pissed up Leeds fans, but Max knew they were well outnumbered. Non-Stop Nigel was lumbering towards them, still a hundred yards up the road. He heard Evrol say "Shit, this is really bad," and released his grip on Stuart. There was only one thing for it.

Turning to face the bouncing tide of advancing lads he raised the pistol and pointed it at the leader, a young lad of about twenty, who sprinted forward, fists clenched and a malevolent grin on his face. Max had banked on the sight of the gun having a dramatic impact on the group's advance. He hadn't reckoned on the effects of two days solid drinking and the fact that flare guns had been used in terrace battles on a number of occasions in the preceding years. It quickly became blindingly obvious that no one believed the gun was real, as Evrol was felled by a flying drop kick to the chest, and seconds later the first punch connected with Max's jaw. Firing live rounds in a city centre within earshot of hundreds of police officers had never been the plan, but as he struggled to stay on his feet under a hail of punches and kicks, he realised he had no choice. Max pointed the gun skywards and pulled the trigger twice.

Chapter 44

"We're en-route control, ETA 4 minutes. Can I have an urgent update please?" Roger Thorpe flicked his cigarette through the patrol car window and used a well soiled hanky to mop the perspiration which was streaming down his face.

"Continued serious disorder, West Undercliff Promenade. Multiple males engaged in violence and unconfirmed reports of shots fired," came the crackled response over the radio.

Thorpe shook his head. Just when he thought things couldn't get any worse. Firearms now. Who the fuck could that be? He'd heard on the grapevine that a couple of the old London boys who'd retired to the coast in the seventies to run pubs and clubs, were seriously unhappy about damage Leeds fans had caused to their property, and having to close on a Saturday night. Maybe they'd called in some favours and brought a few big hitters in to teach these northern thugs a lesson. He also knew that a number of bouncers had ended up in hospital. Handy lads. Some were known to knock out pills to clubbers too. The main dealers wouldn't be happy. Maybe it wasn't such bad news after all. Fuck them. Fuck their hooligans and fuck their West Yorkshire police intelligence. Didn't foresee this in their car boot risk files did they?

The action was over by the time they arrived. Always the best way. Roger Thorpe peeled his white shirt from his back and retrieved his cap from the front seat of the car.

"All contained Sergeant? What's the story?"

"Leeds on Leeds as far as we can tell. Fighting amongst themselves. Got well out of hand though..." He raised a clear plastic evidence bag containing a Glock pistol.

"My God. Injuries?" Thorpe surveyed the scene of a dozen hooligans in shorts, face down, arms restrained by plastic cord ties.

"No gunshot injuries but a couple of them have taken a bit of a pasting. Numbers were against them, the black lad is in a bad way. Also, two of ours are on the way to hospital. This big fella wasn't coming quietly." The sergeant nodded towards a semi-conscious giant, seated against a wall with restraints on wrists and ankles, his face a mask of blood.

"No idea what it was about so we nicked them all. There was a young woman with them too. We took her details and let her go."

"Who was the shooter?"

"No idea sir. The pistol was on the floor by the time we got here. The big guy, the negro and this one with the broken jaw were getting the shit kicked out of them. We probably saved their lives."

"Hmmm. Pity." Roger Thorpe removed his cap and grimaced at the sound of chanting from the beach.

"It's going to be another long night sergeant."

"Sir."

"But this time, it will be them who can't wait for it to end. Tonight we get our payback. No fucking prisoners. Understand?"

"Yes Sir."

"Carry on sergeant. Good work."

Chapter 45

Neil stood at the end of the pier and stared out to the unusually calm waters of Poole Bay and the English Channel beyond. The contrast between the empty expanse of blue ocean, and the beach to his right which was now rapidly filling with groups of chanting Leeds fans, was stark.

With all sources of alcohol closed in Bournemouth, take-out beer had become a valuable commodity, and those who had invested in a beer-run taxi to Poole or Christchurch were now well rewarded, as thirsty fans offered £2 for a single can of lager. Observed by massed ranks of riot police from the beach front promenade, ghetto blasters pumped out an eclectic mix of Indie, dance and LUFC classics from the 60's and 70's as the Leeds fans celebrated their teams' return to the top division.

Neil scanned the beach, looking for Hursty and the rest of the lads, and reflected on the last few years. Watching lads kicking footballs, wading in the sea, cans of ale in hand, celebrating promotion without a care in the world, brought home just how fucked up his own situation was. No house, no girl, no real job. Mother slowly dying in a shit flat, brother on the run with a death sentence hanging over him. Leeds promoted and he was stood on his own, sober and hoping desperately for a meeting that might never happen. For all he knew, Connolly and his gang may have already tracked Stuart down.

"Neil!" A woman's voice caused him to turn from the beach and look back down the pier. Dark hair, yellow top, black skirt. Looked like a primary school teacher. Julie. Face flushed and tear streaked, she stumbled on the pier's wooden decking as she hurtled towards him. Neil's surprise at seeing his mother's helper turned to panic as he caught her terrified expression.

"What is it? Is my mam okay? What are you doing...?"

"Yes, don't worry, your mum is fine. It's Stuart..."

"Oh God no..."

"Don't worry, he's okay, but he's been arrested."

"What? Our kid's been nicked?" Neil's relief manifested itself in an unexpected smile at the irony of his brother being arrested at football. For years he'd told Neil that scrapping at games was a mug's game.

"What are you doing here anyway?"

"It's a long story." Julie suddenly realised how bizarre her appearance on Bournemouth pier must seem to Neil. "The important thing is that Stuart is safe for now."

"I know you." A gruff Scottish accent caused Julie to turn, and for the first time Neil noticed the figure approaching slowly behind her. Greying hair in a frizzy mullet, a black shirt unbuttoned to mid-chest level, the crime against fashion topped off by a cream coloured suit.

"I do know you." He nodded towards Julie. "But I don't know you son. Who are you then, mystery man?"

"I've no idea who this is..." Julie turned to Neil, who instinctively reached behind his back for the gun in the belt of his jeans as the man approached.

"Fucking chaos this, eh brother? The stranger smiled and shook his head, staring into space.

Then turning back to Julie and Neil. "He was coming to meet you. You led us to him. You're a fucking amateur son, whoever you are."

"So you're him...Connolly." The grip of the pistol in his waistband felt moist from the sweat soaking Neil's palms.

"Correct. And may I ask what your interest is in my business affairs?"

"I'm Stuart's brother. He's fucked up, but we can sort this out."

"Did you hear that Keith? The boy's brother, but we can sort it out. Fuck's sake." Connolly's smirk morphed into a spluttering crescendo of laughter which caused him to bend at the waist and turn away from Neil and Julie. A slow pivot brought him back to face them, and now, in his hand was a foot long bayonet.

"Twenty five fucking grand that little cunt stole from me, and now his pals, who I assume are also your pals, have kicked the fucking shite out of my boys and got them all nicked. Big Nigel is on licence so he's fucked, he'll be seventy before he gets out. Wee Maxie's jaw was nearly hanging off, and they'll find his prints on the Glock so he's had it too. And that poor black kid. Your fucking brother..."

Connolly had been advancing towards Neil holding the bayonet when the gun appeared in his eyeline.

"One more step and I'll blow your fucking face off you Scottish bastard."

"Neil, no, please..." Julie stepped forward, arms raised.

Connolly was doubled up again. "Ha Ha, for fucks sake brother, do you think this wee cunt looks like he has the balls to pull that trigger? Nah, me neither."

Julie glanced over her shoulder as the distant drumming of batons on shields heralded the arrival of a hundred strong force of riot police, marching towards the beach in four rows.

"Put the fucking sword down grandad or I'll take your head off." Neil levelled the pistol at Connolly's forehead and tried to stop his hand from shaking.

"You know how to fire that thing son? Is it even a real shooter?" Connolly stepped forward, flicking the bayonet in front of Neil's face as a roar from the beach accompanied a charge from the Leeds fans towards the advancing police lines.

Neil struggled to control his breathing. He'd brought the gun as an insurance policy. He'd never considered actually having to fire it and Scouse John probably suspected he wouldn't need to. Now he was seconds away from that, if it even worked.

"Put the bayonet down, or I promise you I'll pull the trigger." Neil's laboured breathing and shaking hand contrasted with Connolly's quiet confidence and mocking smile, but the desperation in Neil's eyes told the older man that this could go either way. He knew that a scared man was a very dangerous man.

Connolly nodded and smiled and slowly walked to the pier edge and placed the bayonet on the wooden railing, as Neil kept the gun trained on his head.

"Okay son, you win this time. Something you should know about me though. I never forget. So even if I walk away now, the fact remains that your thieving bastard brother has my money, and he has to pay for that."

"Neil, think about it...just calm down, there's no need to do this." Julie slowly raised her hand and moved towards the gun as a huge roar from the beach accompanied a baton charge by the ranks of riot police, which scattered the Leeds fans towards the shore line.

"I tell you what though son. You could end this whole thing right here, and save your brother's life. But only if you have the bottle to pull that trigger. Because believe me, whether he pays my money back or not, that little cunt has to suffer. That's the way it works."

Neil's finger tightened on the trigger and he was surprised to feel his breathing slow and a calmness descend. Connolly had made the decision for him. Everything had become clear. There was no other way now.

"Neil...Neil...please no. Think about it." Julie was alongside him now, a quiet voice of reason.

"I have to..." Neil looked down the barrel at Connolly's smirking face and knew this was the moment his life would change forever.

"You can't Neil. You can't kill him..." Neil's eyes remained locked on Connolly's.

"Go ahead boy, I really don't care one way or the other." Connolly spoke calmly and smiled and closed his eyes as Neil fingered the trigger.

And then Julie spoke.

"He's your dad Neil. Connolly is your real dad." Neil's gaze shifted slowly towards her, and the smirk disappeared from Connolly's face.

"What? What the fuck are you saying?" Neil lowered the gun, so it was now pointing towards Connolly's chest.

"That's why I'm here. Your mum told me. He's your real dad. I'm so sorry Neil. I didn't want you to find out like this, but I couldn't let you kill him."

"No...how can he? How can he be my dad?" Neil lowered the gun as Connolly began to laugh. A low chuckle which slowly became a full throated belly laugh.

"He's my son? Hear that brother? The laddie's my boy!" Connolly shook his head and looked out towards the white sands of Bournemouth beach, now splashed with red as the TSG enjoyed their revenge.

"Who's his ma then?"

"Christine. You knew her as Christine Harrison. He was born in 1965 just before you went to prison."

"Aye? Christine? I remember now. Remember that wee boy. Fuck's sake, I bought you a wee bike for Christmas once." He laughed again.

Neil was slumped against the pier railing, shaking his head.

"I can't believe she didn't tell me. Why didn't she tell me if she knew he was the one who was after Stu?"

"I think she tried Neil, honestly I do. She didn't know what to do for the best." Julie moved slowly to the railing to slip the bayonet behind her back.

"Jesus. So what happens now?" Neil looked at his father, feeling the weight of the gun in his hand.

"Well if this was a movie, I'd no doubt throw my arms around you and say everything's going to be okay. I'd forgive young Stuart for his error and maybe even let him keep my money. He's probably something like my half nephew after all. Then me and you would go for a pint and get to know each other." The smirk had returned to Connolly's face.

"But to tell you the truth son, I've no fucking idea how many kids I've got scattered around the place, so another bastard makes no difference to me. Your brother is still a thieving wee cunt and he's still going to pay for what he's done. So unless you have the balls to shoot your father in the back of the head, I'm going to walk away now. No doubt we'll meet again at some point very soon."

Connolly waved, then slowly turned and began walking, as a cloud of smoke from burning deckchairs drifted across the pier.

Julie placed a hand on Neil's shoulder.

"Forget him Neil. He was never your dad. Stuart's safe for now, that's the main thing."

"Hey darling." Connolly turned, about twenty feet away and began walking back towards them.

"I never forget a pretty face you know. I recognise you."

"I've never met you before in my life." Julie felt a sense of dread at what was coming.

"No, you're right, we've never met, but I've seen you. Your husband carried your photo in his wallet didn't he...?" Connolly swaggered towards them, grinning again.

"Richard? How do you know Richard?" Julie tightened her grip on the bayonet behind her back.

"Let's just say Richard was another business associate who let me down very badly, and he had to pay the price for that." Connolly was in front of her now and she recoiled as he reached out to stroke her cheek.

"No...what have you done to him? Where is he?" Julie felt her eyes start to sting as the smoke drifting from the beach became thicker, and the pounding bass from a stereo blurred into the clatter of police batons on shields.

Connolly ran his hand through his straggly mullet and looked out to the beach.

"Creative accountancy at my expense is a very bad career move sweetheart, and unfortunately he had to learn that the hard way."

"My God, no, what have you done? Where is he?" Julie was sobbing now as Neil gripped her arms and she tried to move towards Connolly.

"Aye, he learnt his lesson right enough. Sounded very apologetic on the phone in the end. Do you know what he sounded like?"

"You bastard. You fucking evil bastard." Julie spat at Connolly as Neil restrained her.

"He sounded like an animal...a cat in fact. Just like a wee cat being strangled." Connolly roared with laughter, turned and waved as he headed down the pier.

"Bye son!"

Julie sobbed loudly and Neil needed all his strength to hold her as she tried to wrestle free. As he struggled to contain her flailing arms he was surprised to feel the cold steel of the bayonet in her right hand, and released his grip. Julie paused to glance at Neil, biting her lip as tears streamed down her cheeks, then followed Connolly down the pier.

Chapter 46

Sunday 6 May 1990-

Thuggery on a Day of Triumph - YEP Special Report --It should have been a day of triumph, but for Leeds United, its supporters and the city of Leeds, it turned into a day of shame. The ugly face of United, largely suppressed in recent years, showed itself again and at a stroke, the club, city and fans were tarnished. Genuine supporters watched in disbelief as hundreds of young men in T-shirts and shorts, many high on drink, charged the police outside the ground, hurling bottles, bricks and stones at officers protected by riot helmets and shields.

Roger Thorpe was surprised to find the glass of whiskey in his right hand when he lifted his head from his office desk, and blinked in the dawn light streaming through the open blinds. He smelt of smoke and cells and blood and cigarettes. The taste of the whiskey caused him to grimace, and he had to light a cigarette to take away the taste. The smell of his own sweat was overpowering and his head pounded to the beat of batons on shields and heads.

Roger Thorpe smiled. Memories of the night before, giving it to those bastards on the beach. The Met TSG really going to town on the northern scum. No prisoners last night. Fuck them. Fuck their West Yorkshire intelligence.

'Contain them on the beach. Dispersal makes no sense.' Fucking Yorkshire police with their risk files and their polo shirts. 'You're losing control. Making it worse.'

Whining northern cunt. His face when Roger Thorpe had told him. He was the Gold Commander. He was in control. Fuck your containment. This isn't dispersal Sergeant, this is fucking revenge!

He was in the 3rd floor washroom, splashing his armpits with cold water when Anderton from CID burst through the door.

"Body on the beach sir. Washed up on the morning tide. Do you want to be kept updated?"

Had to be related to the football. Most likely a drug or drink related drowning but, then again, maybe some of the local bouncers' London re-enforcements had taught someone a serious lesson.

"Give me the location and I'll call on my way home. I need a shave and a shower."

Twenty minutes later, Roger Thorpe was again blinking into the unrelenting morning sun as he stumbled across the sand, shirt sticking to his back, new sweat on old sweat, past the smouldering embers of deck chairs and rowing boats, deflated beach balls, discarded clothing and hundreds of beer cans and bottles scattered along the tide line.

A white tent had been assembled at the point to which the corpse had been dragged, beyond the ebbing tide, and two detectives in shirtsleeves tossed their cigarettes as they spotted him approaching.

"Sir." A uniformed officer manning the blue taped cordon saluted as Roger Thorpe ducked beneath it.

"Shift these onlookers please constable." Thorpe nodded to a bedraggled bunch of bleary eyed beach-sleepers who were monitoring proceedings from a distance.

DC's Cunliffe and Muir had fallen unlucky and taken the call at the end of their shift.

"What do we know gentlemen?"

"Middle aged male sir. Spotted by a dog walker just after seven. The tide was going out, so we had to wade in to retrieve the body." Muir eyed his ruined Barratt's slip-ons and knew there was no chance of Thorpe offering to cover them on expenses.

"You'll dry soon enough in this weather detective. SOCO here?"

"In the tent sir."

Philip Dalton was directing a photographer in taking close-ups of the deceased when Thorpe ducked into the tent. The body was positioned on its back, arms spread wide in a crucifixion pose.

"Good morning Philip, do we have a cause of death?"

"We do sir, and I think it's fair to say it's not accidental."

Dalton pulled the man's jacket and shirt aside to reveal a neat incision in the left rib cage.

"Stabbing then?" Bournemouth's first murder in almost a decade set Thorpe's pulse racing.

"I'd say so. Interestingly, there's an exit wound too, so we're not talking about a flick knife or one of the Stanley knives these hooligans use."

"No? Something bigger then?"

"In my opinion sir, I'd say the deceased was stabbed through the heart using some sort of small sword."

"Poor bugger." Cunliffe and Muir had joined their boss in the tent.

"Doesn't really look like a football hooligan."

"Looks more like an extra from Miami Vice." Muir's muttered comment was louder than he intended and was initially greeted by suppressed smirks, which quickly became sniggers, then full blown laughter. Thorpe coughed to signal an end to the levity, and the five men shuffled their feet and put their hands in their pockets, to silently observe the corpse laying on the sand before them. Alan Connolly stared back towards them with unseeing eyes. No prisoners today.

Chapter 47

Tuesday 21 August 1990

Troops Surround Embassies -- The Gulf crisis took a dramatic turn today when Iraqi troops surrounded the British Embassy in Kuwait. Armed soldiers also encircled six other foreign missions.

Ticket Chaos Fears at First Leeds Match-- Season ticket permit chaos at Leeds United has raised fears in both Merseyside and Leeds that the club's return to the first division may be marred by confrontations with ticketless or non-segregated fans. Club officials at Goodison Park, where United play Everton on Saturday, have expressed concern over demand for tickets exceeding supply, and United's failure to distribute Premier Card permits to all ticket holders. Police fear United fans may end up mingling with the home crowd after buying tickets for Everton sections of the stadium. Leeds have been threatened with a Football league death sentence unless fans clean up their act. The newly promoted club was threatened with being kicked out of league soccer after the FA's investigation into May's Battle of Bournemouth.

"Here's to new beginnings." Neil raised his bottle of Michelob and Stuart joined him in a toast, as the Quantas 747 lifted off into a cloudless Heathrow sky.

Julie lifted her own half a lager. "Bon voyage Christine! And here's to you two as well."

"I never thought you'd pull it off our kid. That night at the Barnsley game, when you told me what you'd done, I knew there was no going back. Thought you'd signed your own death warrant." Neil took a swig of his beer as the threesome watched the plane shrink into the distance on its southern flight path.

Stuart shook his head. "I did a stupid thing. I just wasn't thinking straight, but it looks like things have turned out alright. Mum gets to go live near auntie Diane, away from Holbeck and our shitty weather and that flat, and I got some money to buy a set of proper decks."

"How's Stu's disco going anyway?"

"Fuck off! Actually, I've got a residency three nights a week at a club in Clapham, a night called Soak. They're queuing round the block by eleven. Danno runs a Sunday afternoon chillout session at a bar in Camden and a techno night in Dalston on a Thursday. We're doing alright...looking for a bigger flat as it happens!"

"Staying away from the pills too I hope..."

"Yes Dad!...Well, let's just say I've exited the retail arm of the scene."

"Glad to hear it. It'll fry your brain that stuff you know..." Neil shook his head and suddenly felt like an old man. Strangely, it felt good. He was finally doing what he'd promised his dad in looking out for his younger brother.

"You're not going to Goodison on Saturday then?" Stuart turned to face his brother as their mother's plane finally disappeared from sight.

"Nah. Hursty and the lads are going on' train. Tickets for their end. I can't risk any of that anymore with my new job. Looking forward to getting to a few home games, but I've had it with' aways. Too risky. Got to move my stuff out of mam's flat too at the weekend. Council want the keys back on Monday."

"You're sorted for somewhere to stay though? If you need a few quid to help out..." Stuart smiled.

"Cheeky bastard! I'm doing alright for cash thanks. As much overtime as I want."

"Staying at Hursty's then?"

"Somewhere else." Neil muttered and finished his bottle.

"Where you staying then?"

"With a friend."

"Friend? What friend? You haven't got any friends." Stuart smiled.

"Same again lads? I'll go..." Julie finished her drink and headed to the bar. Stuart followed his brother's gaze as she dodged past a large American manhandling an oversized suitcase.

"Just someone..."

"Yes, mate I think I've got it." Stuart winked and laughed at how he could still make his older brother blush when it came to women.

Julie returned with their drinks. "What are we drinking to then?"

Neil raised his bottle. "To a new decade. The eighties have certainly been interesting, but I think I'll be glad to see the back of them."

The three of them raised their glasses. "To the end of the eighties, the start of the nineties, and new beginnings eh? New jobs, new homes, new relationships...even a new Leeds United, back in the big time at last!"

Chapter 48

Monday 19 November 1990

Drugs Busters Seize Cannabis -- A hundred police officers swooped on a busy Leeds pub in a major clampdown on suspected drug dealers. Twelve people were arrested after the raid on the Fforde Grene pub at the junction of Roundhay Road and Harehills Lane. A number of controlled drugs were seized including cannabis and LSD. Operation Boiler was the climax of a length undercover intelligence gathering operation by West Yorkshire police into suspected drug dealing in and around the pub.

Roger Thorpe stood up from his desk, stretched and rubbed his eyes. The murder enquiry had really taken it out of him over the past six months. Sixteen hour days had become the norm and he seemed to spend more time in the incident room than he did at home.

He poured himself his third scotch of the morning and lit his fifteenth cigarette, as his gaze scanned the long, strip-lit office with its lists and photos, maps of Bournemouth town centre and schematics showing potential routes of entry and exit for the unknown attackers.

Officers busied themselves silently with case meetings; hammering the phones trying to locate witnesses and tapping away on typewriters; logging new leads and closing off dead ends. His team. Hand picked, each and every one. Barry Cowell, Roger's mentor at the academy. George Carr, ex Para, one of the first on the ground in Operation Tonga at Pegasus Bridge. Harry Stephens, learnt his trade from Nipper Read. Old school coppers like him, solving cases using their policeman's intuition, ignoring the bollocks and bullshit of PACE and intelligence led policing.

The brass knew though. The biggest murder enquiry Dorset police had ever undertaken, and he was in charge. Personally selected by the Home Secretary. 'The most competent officer in the Dorset force. 'The commander who won the Battle of Bournemouth', as the Right Honourable David Waddington had described him. The Chief Constable wanted to hand the case over to Scotland Yard, but Waddington had insisted. Scotland Yard and their specialised murder unit. Their computers and DNA tests and fucking intelligence. Fuck them all.

Thirty five years in the force, only two months from retirement now, if they allowed him to go, and that was looking unlikely. When he cracked this one, it was pretty certain he'd be moving upstairs. Then things would change. He'd get the force back to proper policing. Banging heads instead of updating files to be kept in a car boot.

Thorpe picked up a sheet of A4 and read through the words scrawled in his own spidery handwriting the previous evening. The words he'd be delivering live to the nation at a televised press conference later that same day.

'Dorset police remain committed to resolving the unsolved murder of notorious gangland figure Alan Connolly in Bournemouth on 5 May 1990. The task force assembled by myself under the direct command of the Home Secretary continues to make excellent progress on this complex case and we are confident that arrests will be made in the coming weeks.'

Thorpe paused. Keep it high level. Don't give too much away at this stage. Certainly don't allude to the

IRA involvement. They'd find out soon enough when he directed the commando unit which brought down the Provo's high command. Fenian terrorists. Fuck them all.

He gulped down his drink and rested the bottle on the glass to refill it. Not so much spilt this time. As he'd told the doctor, he could stop his hands shaking when he concentrated. It was just that his mind was too full of plans and ideas and strategies. That was why he forgot things. An over-active mind, like all great leaders.

With his press briefing in his left hand and a glass of scotch in his right, Thorpe walked the length of the incident room as he did every morning. Salutes and smiles from his officers, Harry raising the stem of his pipe in greeting. The strip lights flickered and the floor sloped steeply away ahead. Fingers tapped silently on typewriter keyboards, unheard conversations on desk phones.

In the corner of the room, sat on a stool next to the coat stand with its Mackintoshes and Trilbys, a little girl nursed a doll with straw hair and staring eyes, its eyelids stuck open. She pointed as he approached.

"Where were you?" She scowled at him.

"You know I had to work Sarah. I'm sorry." Thorpe smiled but she folded her arms and turned away to face the wall. "You never came. You're always at work."

"Please take care of my daughter, Janet. She's not very well.'

The woman with the tight curly perm looked over her shoulder at him, then turned to point at a folder on the desk in front of her.

"The Chief Super says you need to review the images for the PCA investigation."

Roger Thorpe took the blue plastic file back to his desk and opened it to see a pile of black and white crime scene photos. The first image showed Alan Connolly, laying on the white sand of Bournemouth beach in his cream suit, eyes wide, unseeing, eyelids stuck open.

"My daughter.... please Janet. Can you see to her?" But Janet had gone, her seat now empty, Thorpe sat down and flicked to the next photo.

An elderly St John's ambulance man cowering beneath the flying feet of bare chested, red faced men, chalk dust rising in the sun's rays. Blood on his face, hoof prints on his jacket.

Roger Thorpe drained his glass and turned the photo to reveal the next image.

Four men stretching, next to a black Ford Granada in the car park of Dorset police headquarters. Grinning beneath their moustaches, clutching their weekend bags. Glancing up at the window. Conspiring, undermining, laughing. Fuck them all.

Next image. A small bed in a large ward, empty except for a doll with straw hair and staring eyes.

"You never came." The doll smiled.

Roger Thorpe felt nauseous. Must be those fucking pills. Feeling dizzy.

He closed the file of photos and started back up the incident room slope towards the girl in the corner, his legs feeling heavy now. The desks empty, the task force gone.

"George? Harry? Where is everyone?"

The little girl in the corner lifted the doll towards him. Straw hair and staring eyes, now filled with tears.

"Help me dad."

"It's too late. I'm sorry Sarah. I'm sorry..."

The scotch bottle over the glass, more spilled this time.

"Roger....Roger."

"I'm sorry. I said I'm sorry," Thorpe stifled a sob. He had to remain strong in case the rest of the team came back. Couldn't let them see him like this.

"Are you in there?"

"I'm sorry Sarah. Please darling, daddy has to work now..."

"Roger, come out of the shed please."

"Daddy is working on a big case sweetheart..." Roger Thorpe swigged off his whiskey and sloshed a refill into the glass as he slid down the wall next to the door.

"Roger, open the door please. This has to stop, you're virtually living in the bloody shed..."

"Daddy has a very important job Sarah. I'm sorry but I can't come to the hospital tonight." Thorpe flinched at the sound of his daughter's sobs.

"Roger, unlock the door...please. You're frightening me. Open the door now or I'm going to call Dr. Ryatt."

"Working love. This is very important. You know that." Thorpe spoke calmy and quietly from his position on the floor.

"Come and play with me dad." The girl was in front of him now, still cradling the doll with the straw hair and the staring eyes. "It's not too late."

This time he knew she was right.

"Okay my darling. Stop crying now. Daddy will come and play for a while. It's alright." Roger Thorpe stood and smiled and followed his daughter as she skipped down the long, strip-lit office where his team had once worked.

"What game are we playing?" He washed a handful of tablets down with scotch and laughed as she turned and showed him a rope.

"We can't play at skipping Sarah, not with just two of us."

"Please dad, it will be okay. I promise." Sarah put down the doll with the straw hair and the staring eyes and took her father's hand. She handed him the rope which he'd once used to tow Carol's car.

"It's time to stop working dad. It's time to play now."

"But Sarah..."

"You can still help me. It won't hurt anymore."

Roger Thorpe nodded and smiled at his daughter. He understood the game now. He finished his drink as she waved and began to run down the office.

"Come on dad, you'll be late."

"I'm coming Sarah. I'll be right there."

Roger Thorpe placed a step ladder beneath the wooden beam running the length of the room and tied the rope around it. He put the rope around his neck and smiled as he kicked the ladder away.

Fuck you. Fuck you all.

Printed in Great Britain
by Amazon